AFRICAN WRITERS SERIES

AFRICAN WRITERS SERIES
128

Robben Island

Robben Island

D. M. ZWELONKE

HEINEMANN

Heinemann International
a division of Heinemann Educational Books Ltd
Halley Court, Jordan Hill, Oxford OX2 8EJ

Heinemann Educational Books (Nigeria) Ltd
PMB 5205, Ibadan
Heinemann Kenya Ltd
Kijabe Street, PO Box 45314, Nairobi
Heinemann Educational Boleswa
PO Box 10103, Village Post Office, Gaborone, Botswana
Heinemann Educational Books Inc.
70 Court Street, Portsmouth, New Hampshire, 03801, USA
Heinemann Educational Books (Caribbean) Ltd
175 Mountain View Avenue, Kingston 6, Jamaica

LONDON   EDINBURGH   MELBOURNE
SYDNEY   AUCKLAND   SINGAPORE
MADRID   HARARE

ISBN 0-435-90128-1

Printed in Great Britain by
Richard Clay Ltd, Bungay, Suffolk

Why I Write

I had never wished to talk about the Island. I did not talk about it even to my family. I didn't say we mustn't talk about the place, yet they avoided any mention of it. That is one wisdom I grant them: they recognised my wish not to talk about my life there. It was a strain for me even to think of talking about it. I always felt as if I was crowded into a corner by a ghost, a vicious monster I could not see, holding me spellbound; and like a worm pierced by a pin I writhed helplessly. I remember well the nightmares that hold a man pressed to the floor, while the creature steadily advances. You want to cry out, but no voice comes; you want to kick, but your legs will not move.

And when a man asked about the place, I would feel exasperated; my voice would be choked. I would try to talk politely, but my voice would come out as a growl without my knowing it. I would give terse answers and never explain anything, and my questioner would give up. I am glad my family were not such pests, tormenting my mind after the strain of its torture in prison. Immediately I became aware that I had spoken with a growl, I would spring to my defence. I would say: he who wants to know about the place, let him go down there and find out. I didn't care a hoot about them. They sit lousily on their laurels as if they don't want to be free; they don't want to prosper; they don't want to be human beings. They do this while men are dying on the Island. They would be the first in the queue to pluck the fruits of freedom which they did not help to grow. They would be first to suck the rich juices.

I did not know whom I should address, the businessmen, the intellectuals, the clergy, the students or the masses. The student was the person I always respected: I always remembered the number of students on the Island, whisked off there from the classrooms. My

1

frustration and anger since I left prison was at its height. I had a wound burned by fire in my loin, and any man could come and poke his finger there: of course, I always smiled. Smiled? I grinned. But you can guess the kind of grin that was hidden in my heart, when I felt the pain stabbing up my spine to my brain at such a poke, more vicious than the devil's red-hot soldering iron.

I was happy not to talk about the place, not because of my own pain but because of the grim remembrance of those who remained there. Yet in my solemn thoughts, when I chose to do so, I enjoyed the memory with nostalgic bliss. I had a deep sense of pride. Pride, in a world where pride has been damned as evil; a world where self-abasement and humility are considered virtues, where docility and the slave mentality are revered. Now the man who sits on his laurels would accuse me of pride; the man who benefits from the status quo would accuse me of pride. But pride is merely the appreciation and love of achievement; the recognition of your own value. I would not wallow in the filth of my own dung like a pig: that is self-abasement. I am proud of the fact that I am a human being and that I possess a reasoning faculty, and do not let the colour of my skin torment me like a nightmare. I am proud of the man on Robben Island. He rejected a slave-life. He chose to fight. My concept of fighting is not limited only to action on the battlefield. Fighting means making no surrender to irrationality, not abdicating from one's convictions even when chained to a tree, at the point of a gun. And the warders knew it. There is only one thing to fight in this world: it is irrationality.

You say we have other things to fight besides irrationality? I say no. They may shoot each other in Biafra or Vietnam. But in the nature of things, contradictions do not exist. If you find you are confronted with a contradiction, check the basic facts. You will find one of them is wrong. Either Biafra or Nigeria; either Vietnam or America. If you solve a mathematical problem using two different methods and arrive at two different answers, one of them is wrong. Check your method. Or would you leave the contradiction as the highest form of solution?

You cry out that in the nature of things there are enemies to be fought. I say no. There are only natural resources and energies that cry out to be harnessed. An enemy has a mind, and plots the

2

destruction of man. Inanimate objects and forces do not. You gape at the destruction caused by earthquakes and deluges. Have you ever enquired into the energy in the burning belly of mother earth? You are confronted by typhoons at sea. Didn't you know that it needs accurate mathematical calculation to learn the path of a typhoon, before you plunge headlong into it like a brainless monster? Haven't you ever admired meteorologists? If not, you have no pride in the mind of man.

Don't you admire how the forces of nature are harnessed today—by the mind of man? Can you see the industrial complex; the Ford Falcon you drive in; the hydro-electric power produced by the thrust of waterfalls? No, you take them for granted. You take man's mind for granted—because you have long allowed yours to decay.

If you do admire the work of a free mind, why do you restrain the mind of the black man in South Africa? You give it inferior institutes of learning. You brainwash it to accept apartheid, the machinery of its own destruction. You lock it up on Robben Island.

This is a hell of frustration. I had decided to bar my mouth from telling the story of the place. But I am going to write about it; it is easier that way. It has been a closed book, and now I am opening it.

For various reasons I have written it as a work of fiction. Fiction, but projecting a hard and bitter truth; fiction mirroring non-fiction, true incidents and episodes. The characters are all fictional, including, in a sense, myself.

Going to meet Bekimpi

I went to meet Bekimpi, also called Zweli, after the great African leader.

Only the clutter-clatter of the wheels reminded me that we were still in motion. A rapid clutter-clatter whose frequency gave me an idea of our speed—fast, fast as a swan cutting through the still air.

I dozed. The compartment was full of voices. I looked out through sleepy eyes, not wanting to distinguish the faces. My seat, the floor and myself were immobile, as we responded together in sways and bumps to the bounces of the squeaking carriage, tilting and leaping to the mad spasms of the engine. Everything in the compartment was immobile, but swaying this way and that, everything except the vertical shadows that flashed past the windows. I pressed my nose against the pane. The shadows came from electricity poles passing at the speed of jets. The moment I saw one in front it was behind me, fleeing into the darkness. Everything outside was in motion, the train anchored, at a dead stop. I moved my eyes across the compartment; the eyes about me blinked and glared. Eyes of the rough-and-tumble people, the rank and file, the masses, each one concerned with his own business and his own journey. Among them were spies, of course, spies whose dye ran deep to the inner skin. One had to be careful.

It was a long journey, which terminated in Soweto. Chi came to meet me. A taxi took us away through the darkness; where to, only Chi knew. It was nine p.m. Zulu's juke-box restaurant was still open. We alighted. Some of the boys were there. I looked all around for him, but he was not there. Instead, a handsome young man came forward. 'Chi!' he said, in an excited, girlish voice, 'You're the man I want. Come on, tell me about her. Come, man, jrrr.'

'What do you want with her? Jesus, is this what you came here for?' Chi's earnest voice was a flat denial of the request.

4

'I want to colonise her! I want to extend my colony over her!'

Chi passed by him, throwing him off impatiently. We went into the darker recesses of the location. Now we sat in a dim-lit room. He was there, Bekimpi, standing in front of us, the man I had come this long journey to see. He was the contrast of Chi in physique and temperament. He was huge and short in stature; Chi was lean and raw and bony. He was black, with a broad, flat face; Chi had a lean face and was very light in complexion. Bekimpi had a quick temper, and hate showed in his cruel eyes. He always reminded me of one of the toughs of the Mau-Mau. Whereas Chi was very sweet and gentle.

The room was packed, delegate task-force leaders only. Bekimpi's eyes shone red. He raised his hand:

> Sobukwe sikhokhele, Sobukwe sikhokhele,
> Sifuna 'zwelethu.
> Ngo 1963 so thola 'zwelethu . . .

His voice as he led us was thick and low.

> Sobukwe lead us on, Sobukwe lead us on.
> We want our land.
> By 1963 we shall win back our land . . .'

We chanted in low voices, then listened to what he had to say. He spoke of the lateness of the hour. He spoke of time wasted in speeches and in theorising, of chances lost and wrong decisions. 'So this is Bekimpi,' I said to myself. He was a monster in my dreams. I had known him before, when he came as a vagabond into our location. Now he was very tough. I had never imagined he would become like this.

The keys clanked and rattled as the iron bars swung open. The heavy paw on my shoulder jerked me into the cell. The privy-stink greeted my nostrils, the stink of fresh fart. The lights clicked on as a man rose from a little bucket, pulling his trousers up. A concentrated stink diffused from the bucket, filling the cell, now that the buttocks that had been its lid were removed. The man was disfigured

5

and repulsive. The paw shoved me forward and held me there. The voice above me said: 'Do you know this man?' I looked up at the voice. A tall policeman watched me with vicious eyes, waiting for an answer.

He barked again: 'I said, do you know this man?'

'No,' I said. Only then did I look at the man closely. The short, stout man stood at attention in the middle of the cell, looking at me, full of hate. I forgot the stink in the cell, looking at him. He had a black eye, thickly swollen. The other eye was heavily bloodshot. His mouth was swollen like a cow's, each lip cut and inflated like a bicycle tube. One cheek bulged out as if he had pushed a whole peach into his mouth. His head was covered with ugly lumps. I knew that I could not know this man.

'You know him, bloody Poqo,' the policeman yelled. His comrades filled the door. No, I could not know him. How could I know a man disfigured like this?

'Jong, you'll know him yet. Come along.'

We left the cell. I pictured myself battered into the likeness of that man. My intestines quivered. We entered the torture room. I knew what it was by instinct, and my instinct was right.

I felt my stomach sagging, and my lungs seemed to rise up in my throat. Man, I'm in hell, I told myself. It was an old office, used now as a sort of store room. It was filled with things, ranging from prisoners' jackets to policemen's withered boots. There was a table and a chair. Everything was a gloomy colour, like white paper scorched in the sun. It had the cold horror of a mortuary, the ghostly feeling of a deserted house.

While I was staring at what I thought was the electric chair, someone picked up an empty sack and pushed it over my head. I caught hold of it and pushed back. I was not going to be treated that way, beaten to hell in the darkness of a sack. A struggle followed as I held up my hands, trying to fight the sack off. I felt my body thumped with iron fists. Then there was a voice near the door saying: 'Be careful. Don't do what you did to the other one. There mustn't be evidence of the beating.' I wished the voice would go on, telling the jackals to stop. But they must have heard the voice, because the punching stopped. But then my feet left the ground, and for a moment I was in

6

the air, while my feet were gripped in hands like a vice. Then I was prostrate on the floor. It was easy for them, as I was so small. I felt a heavy boot resting on my face. The voice said again: 'Wait, wait. Not like that. I'll show you.'

There was a moment's peace as the senior man approached. I was panting like a horse. I hoped this man's ways would be softer.

'I'm giving you a last chance,' the man said to me, very kindly. 'All you have to say is that you know that man. Then you'll be free. If not, you'll be beaten like him and go to jail for twenty years.'

My fear believed him, though my mind knew the danger. But my fear could not help me: I did not know the man.

'Who is he?' came the persuasive, fatherly voice.

'I don't know him, honestly,' I said. I spoke apologetically, with cringing respect, as if, if I had known him, I would have hastily spoken his name. But I did not know him and I could not pretend. I ransacked my troubled mind, but I could not remember him.

'O.K.,' the kind man said, 'Hang him.'

This gave me a terrible shock. My lungs hammered in my chest, crushing my throat. I gasped for air. Before I could recover I was handcuffed and lifted up into space and hung on a hook, like a hunk of meat in a butcher's shop. My weight bit into my wrist as the handcuffs supported my body. I was thankful they were not the American self-squeezing handcuffs. While I was comforting myself that I had not been hanged by the neck, I became a punch bag. The fists drummed on my belly; I wished they knew I had stomach trouble that had landed me in hospital not long before. I felt it bursting from a savage punch. My shoe lashed out, and there was a scream which I could not recognise as mine, though I knew I was bleating like a slaughtered goat. I lashed out, while I swung like a pendulum, and my shoe crashed into someone's belly, drawing air from it in a scream which echoed my own. Whoever it was hit me in the eye, and I saw blue light. Before he could follow up with a right and a Cassius Clay hook to the jaw, the senior man caught hold of him. With the twisting of my wrist, my hand squeezed out of the handcuff. It was too small for those big old things. I gripped the iron, trying to support my weight, while my other hand squeezed out. I fell down, and my body went on falling after my feet hit the floor. My body fell

7

flat on the floor. I tried to pretend to swoon, but I was half-swooning already.

'Leave him for now,' the same voice said. It was distinct above the din of growling, angry voices, swearing and threatening. In a last glimpse my eyes saw a confusion of colours, a spectrum cut by a crude prism, and I caught an instantaneous picture of cruel faces: a posse of policemen who had come to witness my torture.

I groaned under a smelly blanket, a threadbare blanket of cheap wool, so thin that you could see through it like a silk cloth. I groaned under this ancient thing, eight years old, unwashed since it left the factory. I had no leisure to consider how many troubled and afflicted bodies had breathed under it. I forgot its acrid lavatory smell, its harsh texture. I forgot everything except my relief from torture. Then I thought of the man for whom I had suffered the beating, and wondered how many of us had been arrested. I thought of his huge body, the fire in his eyes, the broad face that was broader with swelling. The big head in two sections . . . I wondered whether Bekimpi was arrested too. Hey, why did I think of him? The broken nose fitted in. The swollen lips, shrunk to the proper size, they fitted in. How could I have known it was him, messed up like mashed potatoes? Thank goodness I hadn't recognised him, otherwise I might have coughed the name out during torture. I told a lie which was the truth, an honest truth at the time. And the policemen were almost convinced it was the truth. I hoped I would not be subjected to the same experience again.

A sense of relief and happiness stole into my heart like a trickle of ice-cream. A feeling of joy, uncertain as a feather-touch on the brow of one's lover, the feeling that I had not betrayed a son of the soil, that I nearly had but did not. A stoic's determination squeezed my heart: however much they tortured me now, I would be dumb.

With this feeling my consciousness ceased to dwell entirely on itself, and I heard voices in a noisy brawl in the next cell. Prisoners like to converse in scowls. I was alone here. This brought another train of thought: 'Am I really in custody? Have I really been arrested? Is this all fancy or hallucination?' I went out like a candle.

Many things had happened since the last day I saw Bekimpi. And here I was with Bekimpi once more. But I had travelled to meet him for the second time not by train as a free man, but by Special Branch car as a prisoner.

I was new to this kind of struggle, but I had sensed a difference in the climate of affairs. When I opened the window of my political sleep I saw that the air was charged with storm. The storm assailed my window, agitating the curtains of my heart. The land was charged with oppression and police terror, a negative charge. The gathering clouds, dark and grim, positively charged, built up, the prelude to a violent storm. Tension was thick in the air: as Sobukwe said, it could be cut by a knife. Walking in an atmosphere of such tension, my limbs were heavy to lift, as if I walked in a compression chamber. But the forces of darkness, having mobilised, were the first to attack. Before I was aware of it, there were arrests all over the country. As soon as I awoke from political sleep I found I was in the struggle, and as soon as I began to understand the nature of the struggle I was in prison. They descended on me like a pack of wolves on a lamb, heavily armed. To their disappointment they met with a tiny, scraggy man who couldn't hurt a fly. My only weapons against them were my moral courage, my ideas, my love of freedom.

At that time I thought I was the only one taken. But now I knew Bekimpi was in one of the cells. And, thank heaven, they did not repeat their savage methods of interrogation.

The clank of keys and the rattle of the grating woke me with a start. It was a night check, or, I feared, torture again, at midnight. The light clicked on. I saw one, then two, then three, then—I jumped out of bed, terrified, like a man who has seen a ghost. My blanket and mat were red. The floor near me was red. The walls were covered with red spots. The red army was everywhere, on the walls, on the floor . . . My God! My God! When the police came into the cell they found me out of bed, pale and shivering. They saw instantly that it was not them I was frightened of. They asked, in a chorus: 'What is the matter?'

'Bugs! Red bugs . . . bed bugs!' I cried.

They erupted in a noisy laughter that rumbled along the prison walls. I brushed three bugs off my shorts with a panicky hand. The door slammed behind the amused policemen. I had a last chance of seeing the red things disappearing into unperceived corners. Then the

9

lights clicked off. I stood in the darkness, perplexed. I knew that wherever they were they were preparing for a further attack. As I was fresh from school, the first thought that occurred to me was: typhoid, typhus . . . then I thought of a twenty-year term in this company. I felt my nerves vibrating, quivering.

I lay down, slowly, and listened. Soon I heard them falling on the floor with little thuds. I knew they dropped from the ceiling when they were in a hurry to suck blood. Crawling down the wall was too slow for them . . . thud, thud, thud. I sprang up again. I remained standing, I don't know for how long.

Bekimpi was the first to be sentenced. I, later on, when months of trying to persuade me to be a State witness had failed. I first made the journey to Robben Island in August 1964, after taking part in a hunger-strike in the mainland prison at Kroonstad; only six of us out of three hundred were sent off to the Island. We were joined by newly sentenced men from Leeukop maximum security prison, where we stayed on our way to the Island.

The jerking and swerving, the rolling and pitching of the boat made our intestines rise up in the cavity of our stomachs, leaving a vacuum in their place. We felt like vomiting, but no one was sick. This was the first time I sailed in a ship, and saw the sea.

The Island

When we trod the soil of Makana Island, lifting my head I could see Sea Point, and behind it Table Mountain, rising up in beauty and majesty. The mountain had stood there through the ages, and every day fresh history was engraved on its memory. It saw the ships of the navigators, Vasco da Gama and the rest. It saw the landing of the three ships that brought Van Riebeeck and his settlers. Because of that landing, the indigenous people of this land have been accursed through history; because of it I found myself in this place, a prisoner.

The reception was more civil than that at mainland prisons. It was done without fuss. Soon we were walking to the cells, a distance of about 150 yards from the offices. Along the way, stone buildings were being put up. Black men in short trousers without pockets, and khaki shirts, were chipping stones into blocks and dragging them to the builders. Squeaking wheelbarrows were pushed along, full of dry or wet sand. Here, a concrete mixer buzzed at full speed as dripping men bustled to keep pace with it, men wet with sweat as convicts howled and growled behind them. And there, one or two sentries stood with their FN rifles, and others stood high up on lookout platforms held up by four poles.

They were black men I saw, Poqo and A.N.C. prisoners, quite distinct from common-law prisoners. Black men, not because they were black by nature, but because the sun had burned away any lightness of their skins. I could not even recognise Jake, the man I had stayed with for so long in Pretoria prison.

'Hey, Danny!' a voice called out as I marched by. There was a man behind a huge hammer that was falling heavily on a giant chisel. It was Jake. Suddenly I could recognise many of them. This is what the Island sun does, when it starts to reign in the cloudless sky. It opens its furnace doors wide, so that the scorching heat burns everything beneath it, and fish jump out of the overheated pools. Sometimes a sentry dozes off, letting his rifle fall with a clatter on the ground.

We made our way to the cells, jumping over the stones, and walking as if we trod on eggs, afraid to crush them. We jumped like frogs over the hot stones because we were bare-footed. We were thirty-two in number. There were four blocks with four cells in each, all in a big yard with sentry-posts at each corner. These blocks were huge, magnificent buildings, with walls as thick as the pillars of bridges. They had large, low windows with bars two inches in diameter. These four cells made the block look like a thick 'H', the joining line being a passage with doors leading to the cells; the passage had one entrance door. The fourth block had just been completed. This was a completely new prison built by political prisoners living in the old prison and in a sheet-metal prison now occupied mainly by convicts.

When we entered we were struck by the similarity between Kroonstad New Prison and this one, in shape and everything else, except for the thick walls and the bars. It was a new style of prison building, I suppose. We had a toilet room with a modern sanitation system and water taps, porcelain washbasins and cement washing basins for our clothes. Opposite there was a line of cold-water showers. It was a real modern prison. If it had not been for the shortage of water every morning, we would not have got our latrine buckets full up to the lids with dung. But there was no water to flush. It reminded us of the full buckets we used to carry in and out of the cell in Pretoria. We had a weekly ration of soap and change of clothes. The authorities really intended us to be clean.

Then there was the cell itself, a large, spacious room, housing about seventy men when closely packed, all sleeping on mats spread on the floor. The mats were thick grass-rope mats, some new and clean, others old and dirty. We occupied C block, cell 3.

The noise started as soon as we entered. It started with quiet voices, as we looked around and admired our new cell, and others went to look at the toilet room. They exclaimed on its similarity to the Kroonstad prison. Our voices grew louder and louder, until the cell was in a commotion of sound, like a location beer-hall.

'Bly stil daar . . . so!' yelled a warder at the top of his voice. The voice reverberated in the passage, down from the main door where he stood, like a man shouting into a huge drum. We laid off a little, then started again, as each of us selected a sleeping area, some quarrelling about who had picked a corner first. Corners had the advantage for warmth. The noise rose again. 'Bly stil daar . . . so!' boomed the voice again. We ignored it. One of the convicts was throwing blankets at us, one blanket at a time, until each man had three. We could not contain our excitement, mostly arising from the fact that we were at last at Makana Island. We so much loathed being in the mainland prisons, and dreaded being at the Island. But since we were already convicted, and nothing could alter that fact, let us proceed to the place of the martyrs. Our anxiety to be there removed any apprehension about this devil Island.

So the noise rampage went on until we saw the head warder standing at the door. It seemed that he stood there for a long time, saying nothing, hoping that someone might turn his eyes and see him. When we did so, we did it all at the same time; our babbling coming to an abrupt halt. When he spoke, he simply said: 'Een maaltyd,' and walked off. That subdued us a bit. It was a bad welcome. There was only the last meal to come, and the day was gone. So we were to miss our one dish. That is a lot for a prisoner, a big loss. But we did get our dish. Perhaps he forgot, or someone made a mistake.

The huge question-mark remained dangling like a seventy-pound steak in a butchery. What was to be the final fate of these doomed men on this devilish, spookish island where the ghost of Makana is believed to roam and lurk to this day? Their fate could not be finally settled by the falling of rubber stamps in South African courts, declaring a verdict of guilty. It cannot be.

Perhaps the answer is concealed in that legend of the chameleon and the lizard who were sent to earth from the dwelling-place of the Lord. The first bore a message telling the people that they must not die; but it walked too slowly. The second was to tell the people that they must suffer and die, and because it walked faster it reached the earth first.

The answer is not to be found in the tragedy of Ham, the accursed

13

son of Noah. The claim of mythology is that we are his unfortunate descendants. It is true that for three hundred years we have been the hewers of wood and the drawers of water.

At the Island we sat on a decomposing mass of termite-ridden wood which we ourselves had cut from the forest. The first prisoners on the Island, between early 1962 and 1964, really had it tough. They were tied down on a newly demolished ant-hill to feel the wrath of the ants, whose peace had been disturbed. We, who came late in 1964, found that the ants had retreated down into their inner chambers under the ground; only a few were left, and we were not stung so much.

I will mention one ugly incident which took place on the Island. Mr Mlambo, a twenty-year-stretch man, a short man, was made to dig a pit big enough to fit him. Unaware of what was to follow, he was still digging on when he was suddenly overwhelmed by a group of convicts. They shoved him into the pit and started filling it up. He struggled to climb out, but they held him fast. When they had finished, only Mlambo's head appeared above the ground. A white warder, who had directed the whole business, urinated into Mlambo's mouth. The convicts tried to open his tight-locked jaws, but could not. They managed only to separate his lips. The warder pissed and pissed; it looked as if he had reserved gallons of urine for the purpose. From far off we could see showers of urine blown from Mlambo's mouth, as he fought off the torrents of ammoniac liquid, trying to prevent them going down his throat. When the warder had finished, his face was covered with piss. Then vicious blows of fists and boots rained around the defenceless head sticking out of the ground. Some grazed it, some softer blows landed and some savage ones did not. He tried to struggle free, but the convicts pressed down on the ground round his head. He did not cry out or speak. When they were tired of the fun, they left him to help himself out of his grave.

This warder boasted of the books of torture he had read. He intended to put them into practice. Most of the savage acts were committed by him, including the most heinous acts of homosexuality. These were only to be expected in a locality separated from civilisation by miles of sea, with a population of more than 99% of men–soldiers crowded together in barracks with raw convicts to

14

chase around the whole day. Only a few of the warders were married.

When I came to the Island I found there was much debate about the Africanisation of the name of this Island, Robben Island. The name finally suggested was Makana Island, in memory of the first political victim of colonialism. Makana the Left-handed lived in the nineteenth century, at the time of the Xhosa wars against the white invader. He was the first Xhosa leader to be imbued with nationalism, and was banished to the Island by the British. It is said that he attempted to escape, but his boat sank, and he was drowned. But nobody knows the truth of this.

After I had been thirteen days in cell C3, there was a clash with the convicts administering the cell. I was removed with three friends, and we were placed in different cells. I landed in A4, where I spent the Christmas holiday, a memorable occasion. Of my own free will, and unknown to the warders, I left A4 to stay in A2, where one of those three friends, Chris, had been sent. We stayed together for a long time, until I received permission to study.

My ambition on the Island was to study. So I was sent to cell C1, which was called the University of Makana. This cell was for those who had been granted permission to study. Many others wanted to go there. The craving for education was intense. In the other cells, learning—using the cement as paper—was undertaken by those who were semi-literate, and those who had left school at the elementary level. Those who were better educated helped those who were not. The aim was to wipe out illiteracy among us, and build a step to higher education. C1 was the centre of cultural activity: plays, shows and concerts were organised. It may seem that we were on a political picnic; but we paid for it in hungry stomachs. When we were having our concerts, an evening-duty guard would appear outside the window and shout: 'You're making too much noise there. Three meals off!' And we would miss our three meals.

Bekimpi

Of all the men I was eager to see, not counting Sobukwe, Bekimpi was the first. I asked about him. I was told that he was in solitary confinement. That stopped the breath in my throat for a second. That night I lay on my back in the cell, staring at the ceiling. If he was in solitary indefinitely, I would not see him. I sank into myself, thinking back; my ears became closed to the mumbling voices about me. I thought of Chi. I had learned that he had turned against Bekimpi in the witness-box. There were many things I wanted to know. Now Bekimpi was in solitary confinement with a term of life imprisonment on his head. I trembled. Outside the window, darkness stretched thick and vast into the sky. Thudding boots stepped in to switch the lights off and retreated unseen. Darkness fell in the cell like an eclipse of the sun. But farther away in the yard, the giant searchlights kept it at bay, and it remained impenetrable beyond them. Voices in the cell continued to mumble.

I woke up the next morning sluggish and fatigued. I had to go to work. I had been some days in the Island. The initiation was a devil's work in the quarry, which I will tell of. But just now I sought to dodge the quarry span.

'New ones! All new ones to one side,' a warder called. Here it comes, I thought. They are not finished with us yet. I shuffled to the back. There was a lot of moving about and pushing. I moved into a small span bound for the airfield. There was still a lot of moving and pushing. Over eight hundred political prisoners formed into irregular lines. White jackets and shorts in four lines stretched and wound off, disappearing behind the kitchen house. A cluster of small spans bound for other places filled the yard. Among them, my jacket was whiter in its newness. I held my ground.

16

'Yes, out, out! That's him. That's one of them.' A convict held me by the sleeve. I pulled away.

'Out!' shouted the warder, 'Come here. Who said join this span? Come, bloody Poqo.' I came forward. Hell, how did they see me? The warder's hair kept falling in his eyes, and he kept pushing it back, always taking off his cap. His eyes were full of mocking hatred. The almost toothless convict, with his three teeth grinning like a rabbit, jumped about in satisfaction, eager to pick out other stray sheep.

I was put on the spare-diet for that offence. It was a little kulukudu adjoining the solitary confinement cells. I suffered three days of spare-diet in the narrowness of that cell. That was the gloomiest place in the jail. Hunger tore my entrails. Three days of sapping starvation. But on the last day of my stay in there I lifted myself up to the little window of the kulukudu. My bones creaked as I did so. My famished eyes bulged at what I saw. In the big solitary-confinement yard Bekimpi stood facing a warder. He stood still and erect. The warder shook his fist at him in hostile gesticulation. Below them a group of prisoners sat hunched over black stones, crushing them into small heaps. The next moment, the warder's hand cut through the air, landing on the face of Bekimpi in a cruel slap. Bekimpi's face didn't shift at the force of the blow. It was like slapping the face of a statue. Instead, his colour became blacker. Before I was aware of it, sweat oiled my face and my famished bones trembled. A second slap whizzed and struck. Anger burst out in me; I wanted to rage aloud. The warder still gesticulated, screaming something I could not hear. Bekimpi's mouth was locked. His eyes trailed off beyond the warder and seemed to focus on me. I deciphered the pain transmitted from them. 'I will suffer like Jesus Christ. I will die like Jesus Christ for my people.' I remembered his words. And the words repeated themselves in my mind, and sang painfully.

I forgot my own suffering and hunger. In my mind I saw the pain on the face of Christ, saw him looking to heaven and in painful gasps crying Eli, Eli, lama sabachthani? The map of Africa was imprinted on the face of Bekimpi. The continent of strife and suffering. There is a legend of a little boy and his sister left in the dark forest by their evil stepmother. In that dense forest man-eaters roared, snakes

17

hustled through the grass or hung from the trees. Hyenas and jackals yelped and barked. The little boy led his crying sister through the depths of fear and despondency. When the stepmother took them into the forest he had dropped maize grains on the way to form a trail back home. But the birds of the forest had come and picked the grains. So they strayed into the clutches of a giant.

Africa wanted to walk back to civilisation, but had been trapped in a grim forest. Some fellow human beings will not let him.

My mind kept racing. I saw a man on the torture rack, his back slit by a two-inch cane, the cuts opening like when a knife slashes a steak in a butchery. The cuts were on Bekimpi's face, his face that was strained and taut and bursting with hatred. The men who crouched there occasionally lifted their heads.

Bekimpi had known such pain since childhood. All the bits of his life story that I learned made me shake with hate. His father was a hobo who settled down with the Nzobo family on a white man's farm. He worked the white man's fields for the Nzobo family. He brewed their concoction of beer and dug a pit to hide it in. He fed the pigs and watched over the cattle. In return he got food and a place to sleep. It was when his strength was sapped and he was frail and sick that Bekimpi was born, of an illegal marriage. His mother was accused of witchcraft by the Nzobo family and driven away.

Bekimpi grew up virtually a slave of the Nzobos. He was ragged and pitiful up to the age of fourteen, and up to that age he looked after the cattle and never saw the inside of a school. His father died when he was eight. At the age of fifteen he stood on top of a boulder and viewed the limitless land before him. The line of the horizon seemed to be fixed and unmoving on the land, and he didn't know that it would retreat before him however he tried to approach it. He had never before ventured beyond the boundaries of the farm. The desire to fly into the world and face it alone became irresistible. He didn't know what the miseries of a lonely life could be, as a man does not know what it is like after death. But he knew that he would go. And he went—he bolted.

He did not yet have to face life alone, since he discovered his mother in Benoni. She was then a washerwoman, sleeping on the premises of the white man she worked for, so he had no actual home,

18

but he tried going to school, pushing to the secondary school, only to find education as steep a slope to climb as Mount Everest. At last he came as a vagabond into our location, and lived as a toughy.

This is a bitter memory for me, and painful to dwell on. Yet it forces its way forward, and I must tell it to the limit of my endurance.

But now my mind came swiftly back to the prison, in time for me to see Bekimpi pushed back into his cell. He staggered forward, held by the back of the collar. I sagged to the floor, not wishing to see more.

My thoughts were interrupted by the clattering of dishes. My mealie-rice and water had come. I looked forward eagerly to a most distasteful dish. But before the clanking dishes reached my door I heard swift footsteps, heavy boots stamping along the passage. Then the figures passed. Diki was there. Soli was there. Makete also. So was Ndaba, and so was Bill. Men of my cell. What had happened? I shouted at them. Some looked in, as long as the small window would allow them as they passed. They hailed me back, and the warder behind boomed at them. In spite of this, they greeted me with brilliant smiles. I knew they were already sentenced to meal-stop; hence their defiance. But their smiles told me that it was not a serious thing that had happened in the cell. Perhaps they had earned this by noise-making. The footsteps echoed away down the passage.

The clanking dishes reached my door. I was standing there in hungry welcome. A warder held the door open. A dish was pushed in by a convict. Then the door was banged shut, and the bars of the next cell rattled. I was left with my water and mealie-rice. I poured the water out into the lavatory bucket. What remained was about two teaspoonsful of mealie-rice. My belly groaned, and my mind drifted to Bekimpi again.

Bra Black

I wanted to recollect a certain period of his life. He was known as Bra Black then. It was then that I became interested in him. I see once more, his mother sitting on the doorstep of the court-room, wet with tears. But this was towards the end of the period. The beginning of it had been a rough initiation into the facts of life in South Africa, which had a disastrous effect on his character. He was taken for a pass offence, then for a more serious one.

He was a seventeen-year-old boy. He had run a long distance from work, through the centre of the town. He was almost out of it when he saw in the distance a police van lit up by neon lights that hung below the verandah of a large furniture shop. He stopped dead. Even a schoolboy was scared stiff of the police. His elongated shadow fell on something moving in the dark, as he began to retreat. Brass buttons flashed; someone was running. Then heavy footsteps stamped on the ground behind him. Police trap. He bolted. But claws dug into his shoulder, jerking him backward. Two black policemen shouted in unison: 'Pass! Pass!'

'I'm attending school,' he pleaded.

'Tell that to the magistrate,' boomed one cop. In this way he got picked up.

At the police station he told them that he was working as a garden-ing boy after school. When they stripped and searched him, they found particles of the green stuff. The green leaves mixed up with bits of tobacco and crumbs of bread. Dagga, or marijuana. There was a lot of it. Not wrapped, just nestling comfortably in his pocket. Because he was still a boy, he got twenty-eight days with the option of a fine. But this was too much for his ailing mother to pay.

A nice boy among the incorrigibles. A nice-looking boy. At first he was put in cell 1, among small-timers. The next day he was whisked off to cell 5 full of old-timers, the red-jacketed jailbirds. And it was arranged that he was not to be hired out to the farms for prison labour. Bra Kit arranged the whole thing, with the connivance of the yard-warder. Bra Kit was the boss of the jail; as in most jails, a thug bossed all the prisoners. He was a hardened criminal. He was of the type that gets to be boss by bribery, blackmail and brutality.

The horror of prison had played on the nerves of Black. He was a jittering bag of fear. He knew all about the hard life of a prison and all the atrocities committed there, which were told to children with shocking exaggerations. Now, with this nice Bra Kit pretending to be kind, a lion that would protect a cub in a jungle of hyenas, he was full of gratitude. Dishes of well-cooked meat—so rare a commodity —were put before young Blacky. Puzamandla in powdered form—a beverage that had a nice sour taste—made his dish of soft porridge delicious. Kit was a master of smuggling.

This went on for three days. Blacky got the softest jobs, doing nothing in particular around the prison. He was being fattened up, though he little knew it. On the third day Kit began to fondle him in a way that reminded him of stories he had heard, which then had not made sense. Bewilderment, gratitude and fear of what would happen if Kit removed his protection—as he now threatened to do—compelled him to submit. He was subjected to nights of homosexual assault. He found it horrible, and it marked the turning-point of his life. A young boy with a Christian upbringing, whose boyish delinquency had been meddling with dagga, was subjected to nights of terror. The mess of beastly semen, like a mess of jelly on his thighs, was a sight so disgusting as to make him want to vomit. His blood, his nerves, his shrinking muscles, all rebelled against the whole act. He tried to associate it with his own masturbation, to diminish its impact on his mind, but he could not control his revulsion. He became a changed man: he felt bitter, hardened, angry with everything and everyone. He felt as if he could kill a man. He was assailed by visions of blood-letting. He was helpless.

As if God answered his prayers, Bra Kit was selected for a prison draft. Bribery did not help him this time. He said to Foot, almost in tears: 'Protect my kid. I leave him with you.'

Foot was his lieutenant. And no one could have been more pleased.

He did not know that Blacky's mind was made up, to permit no more of such abuse of himself. Nor did he know that more green-eyed wolves around him were hoping to have Blacky for their own. That very night Toughy announced his intention of espousing Blacky, and challenged Foot for him; so did Carvalla. The blood-letting began. An ugly gash on Toughy's forehead ended the brawl. A broken bottle-end had ripped open his head. Foot went to the spare-diet cell. Blacky slept unmolested.

On the following day he made a complaint, requesting to be removed from the cell. The officer, a captain, laughed at him.

The incorrigibles nearly ate him with bare teeth. One spoke out: 'What did you mean by telling the captain? Let me tell you something. The captain was a moffie too, before he was a captain, when he was at the barracks. He won't help you.'

It was true. When a warder has once been a homosexual, as many are in the barracks, he can find peace of mind only when he knows that convicts do it too. What kind of a convict, a kaffir, and a small chap at that, would rebel against this when he, the captain, did it?

So the convicts queued up to have a turn at Blacky, by force if necessary. Under his blanket Blacky clutched a knife. There are many such things in jail. He slept as though cowed. Toughy was the first. He crept inside Blacky's blanket, and barked: 'Hi, sonny, sleeping well?' The next moment he was a pool of blood. He let out a yell; then silence. All was confusion. Blacky stood in a corner, and challenged them all. His eyes emitted fire, but his knees were trembling. The next moment the warders flocked into the cell.

His mother sat on the stoep of the courtroom. She was a lake of tears. Blacky was pushed down into the dock, in that white jacket with 'Further charge' written on its back. He went down with two years for culpable homicide. It was after this that he came to our location and became a toughy.

Six brazen years fleeted by. The memory of Bra Blacky came back in snatches to the minds of the locals, like an insolent dream, a horrible nightmare, bursting out at irregular intervals during the peaceful hours of sleep. The reminder was the actual appearance and reappearance of Blacky in the location during a long series of arrests, followed by release, re-arrest and release again. Since his first murder,

22

Blacky had become a jail-frequenter. He could hardly stay a few weeks outside before being arrested again, on political charges now.

One day in 1960 I was at the local stadium. He broke out among us on the day of that great match. Most of us knew he was out of prison, but the most important thing at the time was the match, and he was out of our minds.

When I reached the stadium the match had already started. But there was still a queue, a double line of more than two hundred people, pressing against each other, fans who impatiently pushed and shoved in the lines. When I looked at the pavilion I saw a host, a multitude of black heads, of white straw hats, of dark brown hats, Stetsons or Dobbs. On the pavilion a cloud of smoke, tiny chimneys puffing white smoke skyward. Now and then an isolated voice rose above the din in hysterical cries of excitement and joy, the voice of a woman. The man with the microphone praised his side, in a voice that became one with the commotion of sound. And the horn of Kid Margo blasted out a kind of Mbaqanga in rhythm with the occasion.

To think that I was standing at the end of the queue when the match had already started made my heart sink in angry despair. This match was the talk of the week. It was paddled by tongues of men in a pool of saliva, as our old people would say. And they needed a lot of saliva, not to talk themselves dry in the throat. The tension could be felt corrosively grazing the tender parts of the heart. Yet few knew that it was going to be the last match of its kind for a long time: the last match of any kind.

Then came the destroyer, with full warning, from the west. What we call colloquially the tornado, whether it is a typhoon, a cyclone, a hurricane or any other kind of storm. I was already in the queue and marching forward; yet it moved so slowly, as many of the courageous, the defiant, the impudent, late-comers, pushed their way in front, cut into the queue anywhere to get into the stadium as quickly as possible. Then there was a sudden blast of wind, a heavy gust, warm or cold, I could not say which; hats flew away from unwary heads. Weaker fans seemed to be blown out of the queue. It was yellow in the west, yellow with dust. It was thick and dense and

23

frightful. It seemed to rest on the coal-mine dumps farther away from the location. Then it was dark; the mine-dumps became one with the darkness and could no longer be seen. Everyone knew that it was coming, and coming fast. Yet people pressed on into the stadium.

Among them another destroyer had arrived. He cut into the line and pushed people away, trying to get in without a ticket, spitting venom. Every time he opened his mouth it ejaculated a tirade of abuse, a language so crude it made the intestines cramp in one's belly. He made menacing gestures and pushed his way in. This was Bra Blacky. No one wondered why he behaved in this way. I had known him for a long time now, but this time I became particularly interested in him. He became the hero of my other half, the untamed beast-self.

When I was inside the stadium at last, I found myself standing next to Beauty. As her name told, she was beautiful—it was not like the ironical contrast of Blacky's name with his handsome physique—and her manner and disposition were beautiful too. But I disliked her. I even disliked her tendency to display a better political awareness than I did. Even now, as we stood there watching the progress of the match, that claimed my full attention, she dared to tell me about the mounting political tension on the Reef. In truth, I had not been aware of it. My attitude towards her had been decided when she hurt my pride long ago, at Daveyton. We had met accidentally at the Daveyton secondary school, during a school match. I was shabbily dressed; not in Bostonian shoes, not in an Aryers and Smith cap; all in all, not in a jongbok outfit. I had none of these things. As she was in better company, with the gigolos of the location known as high society, Beauty turned a cold shoulder on me. Have you observed how a pet dog is hurt by a snub; when it has been happily wagging its tail at its master, its way of saying welcome home; when, after jumping around, with its dusty feet jumping up to touch the newly dry-cleaned suit of the master, it is shoved away by a well-timed kick? At home Beauty could tolerate me, but not in better company. Her way of starting it was an attack on my hair: 'Why didn't you comb it?' she would ask coolly, and desert my company.

But on this day I was more cunning, and I wanted nothing of her. And there was Bra Blacky, my senior by three years, spitting venom in the sports ground, until his eyes fell on the few Europeans watching the match. 'Is this the way of apartheid?' he yelled. 'You Boers, we are going to kill you!' Everyone was shocked, the whites most of all. But Blacky was not a politician; he did not know anything about that. He was just bitter: since the day of his first arrest, he had laid all the blame on the white skin. Unfortunately it so happened that these whites were friends of the location superintendent. These were the only whites who occasionally attended soccer matches in the location, claiming to be the patrons of 'Bantu cultural activity and growth'. Blacky did not know this. All he knew was that whites were the tormentors of black people.

Now Blacky came towards us. I looked straight ahead. He stopped next to Beauty. 'Hallo, baby,' he said, putting his hand on her shoulder.

'Ah, cut it out, you.' She savagely brushed his hand away.

'Oh, you're the type.' He was speaking in the Tsotsi dialect. 'Eh, baby, eh, cheap thing, eh . . .' I was becoming embarrassed, and so were other people near us. 'Look, little girl, or are you a teacher? Look, little teacher . . .'

'Ah, cut it out, you.'

I had never seen such defiance shown by Beauty before. It shocked me. She just looked straight at the field, her eyes burning with anger. I must admit I was jittery. I sensed that I was wholly involved. At any moment this thug would unleash a vicious blow. So I ventured: 'Bra Blacky, don't worry a daughter of the soil.' I was appealing to his feelings of patriotism, because I had just heard him abusing the whites, and I tried to grin.

'What, daughter of the soil? What is that, eh, eh?'

So I only succeeded in drawing his attention away from the girl, to me. Obviously the girl was embarrassing him, and I was the right person to be bashed in the jaws.

'Look, Blacky, I don't want to hear all this dirt.' I tried to be stern; I was not going to be degraded in front of Beauty, of all people.

'You, Danny, you think you're clever. I will kill you.'

I saw that I had given him a shock. I had forgotten that he had, not long ago, interfered with a distant cousin of mine, a drunkard cousin. Because I did not intervene, he thought I had given tacit consent, yet

25

I did not care a damn. He remembered this, and now he was backing away: 'You, Danny . . . you, Danny, you're full of dung . . . dung.'

No one knew why he did not bash my jaws; even Beauty was surprised.

'Don't interfere with other people's troubles, you fool,' she said to me, when Blacky was shouting away down the touch-line.

'I thought he was a son of the soil,' I said.

'Son of the soil, my head,' she said, and looked straight at the field. I swore to myself that I did not understand this girl.

Apparently the tornado changed course. It only grazed the location. Later on, damage was reported in areas that had lain in its path.

When I reached home I was still fretting about something that had seemed wrong in Beauty's handling of me. I spread the previous day's newspapers out in front of me. It was not surprising: now I saw it, something I had overlooked.

My interest had been primarily in the sports pages. Now my eyes raced over the lines, and rested on a picture of a man addressing a crowd. I was fascinated. My eyes raced on again, starting from the beginning this time in a desperate attempt to understand what had been said; and then they stopped on the picture once more. At last I became familiar with the man whose name was printed below: Mangaliso Sobukwe. I read once more what he had said:

'Sons and daughters of the soil! We are on the threshold of a historic era. We are about to witness momentous events. We are blazing a new trail, and we invite you to be, with us, creators of history. Join us in the march to freedom! March with us to independence! To independence now; tomorrow the United States of Africa . . .'

The speech went on to analyse the political situation in South Africa, and it seemed to me that the attitude of the Africanist towards people not of African origin had never been so well explained: the rejection of the idea of dividing the human species into racial groups; the only thing to be recognised being the observable physical differences due to geographical factors.

Suddenly the significance of what Beauty had said about mounting political tension on the Reef dawned on me. Suddenly I saw the tornado in a strange perspective. The winds of change predicted by

26

Premier Macmillan the previous year had never touched our township. Now they came in a cyclonic reality. And Beauty was there. She heard him speak. I heard only the echo of what was said. She saw him, and I had seen only his reflection.

The flushed principal patrolled the corridor. I could not understand what was biting him; he behaved as if termites had been shoved down his back. His eyes were flaming red with anger. The students spoke in murmurs. I heard something mentioned about a secret movement in the location. This did not make sense then in relation to the teacher's anger, until I spotted, written on the boards and the walls: AWAY WITH THE PASSES. DOWN WITH NAZISM. AFRICA FOR THE AFRICANS. AFRICANS FOR HUMANITY AND HUMANITY FOR GOD.

I could not tell who had written them or when. I looked at Beauty; both of us were doing Form I. Again she broke the news. She came towards me, agitated. 'He has done it! He has done it! Sobukwe has marched!' I gaped. 'And the bastards have reacted in the way expected of them. Savages . . . they shot our people in Sharpeville.'

I was sweating; the principal was looking at us from a distance, straining his ears to hear.

'How was the history test?' I asked, trying to change the subject.

'History? You call that history? That piece of indoctrination?'

I realised I had made the situation worse. She went on: 'You, Danny, you disappoint me sometimes. What is this about history, when I was telling you about what has happened?'

'Yes, but don't you see that man over there?' I directed a sharp eye towards the principal.

'Let him climb on top of the school roof and tell them all. Let him tell the whole world.'

Now I was walking away down the corridor, but she walked along next to me.

'I tell you, more Dingaans will be born; many more Makanas, and many more Moshoeshoes,' she was saying.

Once away from the principal I felt better, and I talked with ease about the burning issue.

'Your fault, you Danny, is that you're a coward,' she said.

'You call that a fault?' I said. I did not feel ashamed. Perhaps she

27

was right; but I told myself I was exercising caution. I had always wondered why this girl liked me when there were so many boys in Form III to talk with; perhaps those who had written the slogans that were glaring down from the walls. But on this day I found that she respected my opinions, even though she did not spare me, out of her convictions. When I got down to serious talking, she listened. She was a crack student in class, but was always held in check by me. She would vow to beat me into first position, but found herself trailing second after me. We had been together from the primary school.

The Sharpeville massacre—1960. The arrest of Sobukwe. The state of emergency. Then the writings on the wall, all over my location. The cloud fell over South Africa, and more thickly and terrifyingly over my little township, which was not actually in the limelight of the upheaval. Then a strange creature crawled through the location streets. It was the first time I had seen such a thing. Something like a rectangular tortoise on wheels, the head that peeped out of the block was a gun-barrel. It was on a Sunday morning when I saw them stop at the sixth house from my home. It was a contingent of para-military police, heavily armed; behind them moved these creatures, part vehicle, part tank, part tortoise. Along the street, a line of stunned people leaned on their fences. Fear was an animal that crept into the hearts of many, and their faces recoiled into themselves as if they were being submerged in a bowl of castor oil. In the middle of a pack of uniformed and heavily armed swaggerers walked a man with a deepset worry on his face. They pushed him into a police van. The Saracens roared away. Somewhere in the location they stopped again, picked up another man; somewhere else they stopped once more, picked up another.

In a matter of an hour the location was swept, crosswise, zig-zagged with Gestapo thoroughness. They rampaged through it like a pack of wolves let loose into a sheepfold. Throughout the country the emergency regulations were like a tightened rope. The Saracens had appeared, marking a definite change in the struggle for libera-tion. The white man retreated into his laager, now built in granite, gun-barrels pointing at the African wilderness. A permanent tension had been created. Whites slept with guns under their pillows, and at the sudden barking of a dog guns were clutched by feverish hands;

28

and a mischievous shadow that followed its owner as if it were a separate entity would receive an ill-timed boot. The whole thing was started by a call to positive action against the pass laws. And now the African was left with no alternative but to forego any demands for concessions, and to grab the land by the one way open to him: to blast the granite walls of the laager with artillery fire, since no human tears can demolish them.

The Saracens had appeared. And by the time they pulled out of the location, another man had been pushed into the pick-up van. My notorious hero was gone. I realised that his outburst at the stadium a few days ago had been disastrous—it had been like diverting a mountain stream towards one's home at the foot of the mountain. Bra Blacky was gone. And I could not help exclaiming: worry no more, countryman, for there you will meet with men of integrity. No more shall you meet with incorrigibles, because political prisoners do not mix with them; not because the whites have recognised the humanity of such a separation, but because they fear the spread of political thought to a most dangerous member of the human species, the incorrigible criminal. Go well, fellow-African: the chances are you will come back a better man.

The Quarry

I had had a mind-drift, such as happens in the spare-diet. A drift of the mind, like a sea-ripple from sea to shore and from shore to sea. The lean strip of light rose up the wall, vertically, like a barometric level. I watched it leaving the floor, climbing higher and shortening. It shortened until it became a horizontal dash and vanished. I knew the sun had set, and I prepared for my last sleep in the kulukudu.

Then came the problem of work again. In the kulukudu I did not work, no one did. But outside it was a yoke on our necks. It was a nagging blemish that had come to stay, right on the nose tip. I fitted into the routine. The first day was bitter, as I have said. There was lights-on, early in the morning. And always, when I rubbed my eyes open, the cell was yellow with light and the twilight outside was chasing away darkness. Then the bell, cracking to raise the ceiling. Then the heavy head that felt anchored to the ground, unable to lift up. A shrilling shout of the slogan from a corner, and a drumming response filling the cell. Then echoes of it repeated in other cells. The gymnasts already sweating in the bathroom. A cold shower hissing down on shrinking bodies. Then counting. Then a line-up for food. Then it followed—oh, work!

We set out for work. We were pressured by routine, by a routine laid down by the unkind hand of fate. A routine more severe than that of a rooster with the unerring memory that as the day breaks, it must crow. A routine more base than that of an alcoholic, who involuntarily wakes at midnight for the bottle of vodka, takes a gulp and belches, takes a gulp and farts, takes a gulp and belches and falls dead on the blankets, only to wake up an hour later and repeat the process. A routine more back-breaking than that of a donkey which knows that the morrow means the pulling of a heavily loaded wagon and the whipcrack on its hide. I was a member of the big span, not for long, but I was both tired and bored.

The initiation span for all newcomers was the quarry. So we were ushered into the big span. We were walking somewhere at the rear, we newcomers, so that we did not see where the road was leading us. It was a four-column moving mass of white, more than 500 living men. We broke into the quarry as a man breaks out of a thick mist to confront a blank wall. On our right was a ghastly donga—a ditch —half filled with water. That was the old quarry. On our left, another donga with huge black rock. That was the new quarry.

It was an ominous sight. Ominous because of the preconceived notions that had wormed their way into our nervous systems, turning them yellow. Ominous because we had thought it daring to place a foot on an ice-block and smile; because the island was no other place but the quarry, not the cells, not the ugly vegetation: the quarry had become symbolical, the graduation centre: torture and the island, suffering and the island: we thinking it daring to be there. We had no illusions, we knew there were worse places in the world, worse than Siberia, worse than the concentration camps. We had looked forward to the quarry.

In front of us was the toolshed, and the big kraal where the prisoners were locked in during lunchtime. A few yards away was the sea, cool and green, and then pale blue where the ripples of the tiny waves were struck by feeble rays of the sun. The water seemed motionless, only a thin plastic layer spread out on a continuous plain, that heaved and puffed and sucked, stretched taut and relaxed in shallow widening corrugations. Farther away, the waters were under thrust and suction, and leaped in mighty waves whose strength was always consumed in the cool water near the shore. The shore was spread with yellow rocks and large, dirty green sea-plants. And there were patches of stagnant water that were a repulsive frog-green.

The old-timers had started working while I looked around; and now the newcomers were called. 'All the new ones to one side!' said a strong, good-looking warder. The criminals imitated him, not meaning to sneer, but soliciting for the highest favours. They were a few convicts called the backliners.

'There are your lorries,' they yelled, pointing at rusted, squeaky

31

monsters that were once wheelbarrows. 'No, no, leave those alone!' they shouted, when we rushed for the rubber wheelbarrows. 'Those are yours, there.'

The warder said it too: 'Come on, leave those.' We left them. We had started working. In and out of the quarry. We carried stones that were not wanted and dumped them over on the shore, as if reclaiming the stagnant patches of water.

'Jong!' exclaimed Eddie, 'We are in the shit here.' A short, stoutish young man. He said it with a smile that was always full and contemptuous. He had a look as if he was pushing his nose against an ice-plate or a hot soldering-rod. 'Look, lidoda, if that snout pokes his snout at us, let us fix him.'

'Sure, lidoda,' I said, aware that this was a plain statement that required no answer or question.

He went on: 'I am told he is the shit here.'

So I had been told too. We did not need any persuasion to believe it. He had pointed to Dum-dum.

'So this is the Island,' remarked Chris to no one in particular. 'Damn these new clothes. Otherwise I would lose myself in that bunch.' He was pointing at old-timers working with spades. In the new jackets that had no inside lining, and the new shorts, we were glaringly conspicuous.

A train of barrows came out of the quarry laden with heavy stones which we dumped in the sea. We had started together, following each other, but before long we were meeting and passing each other on the way like cars in Eloff Street. We did not have equal strength; and some deliberately slowed down, while others wanted to be in front, because Dum-dum was at our heels. I looked at that little man, with an oversized forehead that was the first thing to appear every time he entered a cell; a little man with the buttocks of a woman, and with a toothless mouth that made him talk like a child learning to talk. He was a member of the Big Five gangster-pimps of the jail. And the whole of the gang was barking with him, at us, about us and all over us. They were liked by the warders because they were the principal spies.

I pushed the wheelbarrow until my hands were blistered. There was no rest. We pushed the load of stones and dumped them in the sea. I pushed my full loads from the depths of the quarry, up a sandy path that led out of the quarry. The barking and howling of those incorrigible criminals still sounds in my ears even today. I looked at those fellows and swore to remember them in future. Twice the barrow slipped from my grip as I tried to climb the steep sandy rise. When one is desperate for strength no one can say where it comes from. I tried it when I got out of prison to check that I really had that strength, but it was no longer there.

Doing any piece of manual labour at a human pace is good; but doing a mule's labour at a mule's pace is something else. The yells rained down harder: 'Come on, come on, black bastards . . . do you think this is a picnic? Do you think you are in a hotel? In your mother's home? Come on, kaffirs, come on, baboons . . . push, push, push . . .'

Our brothers were now used to the quarry. They talked nice things to us, and urged us to relentless perseverance. They had gone through it too, worse than this. Their ordeal had culminated in a savage 'carry-on' before we came. It was savagely administered by the Boers. The prisoners were ordered to run round inside the yard of the zinc-jail. To run fast, touching the four corners of the yard. The warders lined up, batons in hand. They were raw Boers determined to unleash their raw hatred on the Poqos. Their wrath was like that of a sexually over-charged bull, that has been locked in for months, and is now determined to leave no Poqo unturned on its path to a cow. Indeed, they had lived in barracks for months with little contact with the outer world. They were bulls shown the red, and the red cloth was sewn on the running prisoners. They lashed out at the panting prisoners. They lashed out with the heavy batons, screaming: 'Where is Leballo now? Where is Sobukwe? Where is Nkrumah?' They lashed indiscriminately—on the head, ribs, shoulders, buttocks, stomach and arms. Every time the baton landed, it landed with a sickening sound. All the prisoners could do was to avoid blows that would be fatal, and that made them run all the faster. The captains and the lieutenants stood watching, and at the sentry-posts stood the ones in military caps with FN rifles. The alleged crime was that the prisoners refused to work. There were many warders, new faces brought as reinforcements from the mainland.

The quarry had been mechanised by bringing in a power-digger engine, a water-pump and two lorries that carried the slate-black stones to the builders near the docks and the jail. Half a dozen hardened criminals were sweating behind the massive diggers, nicknamed the jumping-jacks. The whole earth trembled as if there were an earthquake when the jumping-jacks started to work. The wrinkles on the jail-hardened faces of the convicts vibrated in ripples corresponding with the earthquake-tremors. A number of political prisoners stood with huge hammers, striking huge chisels into the cracks in the rocks. They beat in harmony, hammering to the rhythm of a traditional song of the Xhosa warriors. Every time the hammers landed on the chisels, the earth shook.

A great number sat at a distance from the quarry with small hammers, breaking small stones into smaller pieces. They sat in five or six rows, each row with about thirty-five men or more. They sat close to one another, a spread-out mass of white jackets. In front of each was an ant-hill of crushed stones the size of gravel for a tarred road. Between the rows, wheelbarrows were pushed, carrying the stones for the crushers. The hammers hit rapidly with a rat-tat, rat-tat, tat, tat. Somewhere else sang the music of the picks, as they struck the ground simultaneously. They were struck to the rhythm of some traditional song; swung and spun up and left hanging in mid-air, to be clutched again and strike the ground in time with the rest. There was a line of about fifteen men with picks; in the distance I saw flashes of light cut through the air as the chrome-shining tips of the picks were swung in space. Some of the songs derided the warder looking on. One man led the song in Afrikaans, the rest followed in chorus. In English it went like this:

Solo: Hello, my baas, what is wrong with your head today?
Chorus: It is mixed up, crazy.
Solo: You stand and look on, what is wrong with your head today?
Chorus: It is mixed up, crazy.

The warder could not catch the words of the song, though they were in Afrikaans; he was lost in the magnificent display of the picks at work and the beat of the song. Sometimes colonels would come to watch the performance. One Xhosa song went like this: this snout of a white man wipes the mucus off his snout with his tongue.

Somewhere else, shovels and spades glinted in the air, scraping up crushed sea-shells from a cleared space. Everywhere there was a bustle and a din, with convicts running and yelling, doing nothing in particular but flying around like flies with no purpose. The day was longer because we longed for knock-off to come quickly.

When at last it was knock-off, I was dead tired. The big span was again on trek, back to the prison. There was always more dust on our way back, as the weary prisoners dragged their feet on the ground. My exhausted flesh and bones needed more oxygen, and I gasped for fresh air in the thick dust. I walked with my eyes almost closed, and my eye-lashes were full of dust. I just pushed my foot forward to where the man in front had just dragged his away.

In the cell I lay like a log. When it came to the singing of the national songs, I just yawned them out. We sang the songs to mark the end of the day. In the other cells there was singing too. One could not help feeling inspirited and rededicated when such songs were poured out with intense feeling and conviction: songs such as the Zulu one:

> We the brown nation,
> we are crying for our land,
> we yearn for our land
> that has been taken by the white man.
>
> We, the sons of Africa,
> we are crying for our land.
> Let them leave our land,
> let them get out.

The note of pain in this song seemed to remain hanging near the ceiling. Its sweet message reverberated in soft echoes in the walls of the prison, and I felt it fill the chambers of my heart. This was our much-needed food. We fed our spirits, fed them to the point where material food did not matter so much.

The following morning some of us tried to dodge the big span.

35

Around us a number of smaller spans were lined up at the gate. These small spans were for those with shorter prison terms. All the same we were pulled out and marched off in the big span again, cursing our new clothes. Surprisingly, some of us were no longer as keen to visit the quarry as we had been. In the quarry I exchanged my new jacket for an old one, with an old-timer, and disappeared among those who sat, lazing, as it appeared, crushing the small stones smaller, and the smaller stones smaller still. They crushed in a leisurely way. They were sitting on bricks the whole day, doing nothing but crush stones. That was quite easy . . . I put on a pair of wire-gauze goggles to protect my eyes from the stones that shot up like jets as one hammered. I sat between two expert crushers from the Cape. I hit and hit with the hammer, crushed and crushed until my arm was aching. When lunch came, I had made a little heap of stones. I crushed again and again until I felt the muscles of my arm stretched taut to the point of snapping. Two hours after lunch the head-warder came on a round of inspection. He saw my little heap. The next moment his cane landed on my head. I jumped up. He ordered me to sit down and work. I sat and worked. My molehill of stones was dwarfed by the giant anthill of my neighbour. I looked ahead of me; two newcomers who had joined me in the same manner were having the same trouble. 'You have to get used to the job,' the neighbour said. 'Your hand must be strong first. It is just like when you go to a gymnasium for the first time.' To save me from meal-stops, my neighbours gave me many of their crushed stones so that I had a larger heap.

Long after this, when I had got used to the island, I would leave my Hodoshe span and visit the quarry. To spite the warders, I sat with the crushers, and crushed as lazily as I could. When it was time for checking, I would place big stones below and cover them with the little ones I had crushed, so that my heap became a giant hill. There were many such tricks to outwit the warders. In the end the warders discovered these tricks, but new ones were always invented.

After the first disaster at the crushers, I left them and joined the pick team. There I was at home. Two warders watched us pick-axeing, just as the crushers had been watched by two warders. The warders sprouted like mushrooms all over the quarry.

A week later I succeeded in leaving the big span. I joined the Hodoshe span. The quarry is fenced now, and the road to the quarry is also fenced, so that there are men who are doomed to live between fences as long as that quarry is worked, and as long as there is no political change in South Africa. These are the ones with long sentences. They work only in the quarry. Leaving the fenced prison yard, they walk in a fenced tunnel right to the fenced yard of the quarry. I helped in building that fenced road. How could I help it?

The Hodoshe Span

       I walked in the new span. It was a good feeling. I almost felt happy.

A little white-painted house materialised from behind some trees, as we followed the tarred road leading to the village occupied by white warders. It stood a little way off the road at our left. Two sentries stood at the corners of the yard, sometimes taking a step or two up and down, obviously bored. The FN rifles were sometimes raised and lowered at a whim of their bearers, expressing their impatience at waiting there for days and months, watching the man who would not run away, so that he could not run away. Two or three convicts in for common-law crimes quietly worked in the garden. I could not tell how many rooms the house had, for we did not dare to come anywhere near it, or talk to its lone occupant.

We had been walking now a distance of about 800 yards from the main gate of the prison. The road from the gate as it ran along the fence was untarred. It had shot particles of dust into our eyes as some of us dragged our feet in the sand, raising up a mist of dust which engulfed us wholly. 'Lift your feet there, forwards!' our span warder would shout indignantly, his voice rising in a crescendo. Our men would continue to drag their feet until we reached the end of the road where it connected, almost at right angles, with the tarred road from the docks, passing in front of the prison offices down to the village. This road passes through an avenue, a jumble of forest trees that was supposed to be a plantation. Sometimes motor-cars would pass us on this road; sometimes they contained colonels or lieutenants. 'Ka . . . tsof!' our span warder would yell, as the officers approached. He yelled aloud, not just for us to hear, but so that the officers passing should hear his command: a promotion might be on

38

the way. We would parrot him, 'Ka . . . tsof!' when the officers had passed. Actually he meant 'Caps off'.

When we approached the house we were filled with expectant joy, and from behind the window of the house a smiling face would appear, both hands waving vigorously, then steadying to make the best-known hand signal. We responded by raising our hands, palms opened, and this annoyed our guard.

Every time our span of twenty approached that place on our way to work an inexplicable feeling of joy filled our hearts. Anxiety and worry were banished, suffering and toil forgotten, regret and self-pity condemned as traitors to our cause and pushed into the dungeon of accursed fire.

Then our minds would be filled with visions, and we would see the new Africa we so much yearned for and suffered so much for, as if it were just around the corner. All we needed was Noah's dove coming on its return flight to tell us that the waters had sunk and the land was now habitable. What we needed was a peephole, to see if the hyena that had so aggressively charged our castle of retreat had left. We needed to see the silver lining on the dark cloud of suppression that hung dangerously over our heads. What we needed was hope. We felt revitalised and rededicated, because the man who occupied that house was none other than the one most loved by his followers, Robert Mangaliso Sobukwe.

This little island, a mere dot that sometimes does not even appear on the map of Africa, had been hitherto unknown to the man in the street, or brushed aside as unimportant. When Sobukwe set his foot on its soil as the second exiled man in the history of Robben Island— the first was Makana the Left-handed—it was a prelude to the intensified activity of repression which put the Island on the map of the world. Its name, uttered by the tongues of men and women, flew like a rumour, faster than local newspapers could carry it. It was a report of evil omen: the sons of men were now sent there to languish in pain and perish unknown to the world.

The Island was a leper colony that had been converted into a prison for common-law criminals. Already by late 1962 it had housed political prisoners. Sobukwe followed after finishing a three-year sentence in 1963. That opened the flood-gates to a repression similar to that of Stalin when his opponents made their way through the Siberian snow to perish in the salt-mines.

It would be difficult for anyone to understand the importance to us of the presence of Sobukwe on this desolate Island, unless he changed places with someone doing a ten-year stretch or doomed to a life sentence, with the biting Antarctic cold as a background, and with human hyenas—representatives of the regime that had shoved us into this dungeon—for company, not forgetting the growl of the empty stomach besides.

In the first week of our stay on the Island my group had a burning desire to see our Prof, as we called Sobukwe. The chance came our way on Sunday. 'Kerk, kerk!' a convict shouted in the passage of C block, where we were staying. We sprang up at the opportunity. We had already been tipped off that the road to the church passed near Sobukwe's hut on its way to the village. 'Two twos!' the convict said, as we scrambled outside the block into the yard. We were joined by others from other blocks. But we were only a small number compared with the great number of convicts from the zinc jail.

I call the common-law criminals convicts to differentiate them from us. Most political prisoners did not go to church, not even though it offered them the chance of seeing the Prof. They had seen much of him in the past months, and others still saw him on their way to work. However, those who went to church did so merely to see the Prof in passing. Even the convicts had learned, perhaps by intuition —since we did not bother to share our hopes and aspirations with them—to cherish the incongruous hope that their five-to-eight- or nine-to-fifteen-year or life sentences would wither away when that man in the lonely house decided to act.

Robben Island results from some geographical accident that separated a small piece of Africa from the mainland. The notion is held by the majority of its occupants that it got cut off through long years of erosion. A huge question mark hangs about the Island; sometimes it seems to shine brightly on the walls of the cells, or dangles over the heads of the prisoners. It weighs most menacingly on the victims of solitary confinement, or those suffering from T.B. or asthma. The prisoners seek an answer to it: whither Robben

40

Island? Whither Makana Island? You, Island, are a damned ship sailing the dangerous seas, through the typhoon. But you have souls on board, bondmen of the slave-ship, chained to the benches even during engagements with enemy ships.

Perhaps the answer lies in its thick palpable mist, through which a bird cannot find its way, but knocks itself against the walls. The mist is a daily visitor to the Island, every morning. When there are clouds, they are dark clouds, not bringing sudden storms but a patience-devouring drizzle that can wet a cat through to its skin, so that it cringes and groans from the biting, frozen air of the Antarctic. The ever-banished sun time and again peeps through the blanket of black cloud to shoot its rays of hope to the benumbed prisoners.

Or perhaps the answer lies with the sun, since the sun is the symbol of God, and must know why God took away the warm blankets of the condemned. The ice-age came, opening the gates to the dreadful gale of cold whose abode is the Antarctic. It preys with impunity on the bare skins of the prisoners clad only in khaki shirts, khaki shorts, a khaki jacket with no inside lining and a jersey. This last is much loved by the prisoners. We start calling for jerseys as early as February, but they are given to us in April. Winter is long. It may start in March and go on until October. It can be severe, leaving us hunched up in the shape of the legendary apeman, the neck disappearing into the shoulders, and the head looking like a pumpkin placed on the cut trunk of a tree that still stands with its roots in the ground. When we were in span, you could see a disorder caused by our failure to form neat lines. Every one of us avoided the flanks and front, so that he might be shielded by others from the charging cold wind. In the cell, we wrapped ourselves with blankets like sick men in hospital, and studied or talked the evening out.

The summer is short, and its brilliant warmth is always marred by the hated rain. Why does the damned rain not fall where it is wanted and will be of use, on the drought areas of Botswana and Sekhukhuni land? Small showers that send an itch up the spine, and with their incessant splatter set up a solid nagging in the head, like that of a drunken husband pestering a wife who has been peacefully sleeping.

We have seen the mole and a curse has befallen us. There is a

41

time-old legend that he who sees the mole shall hear of a friend's or a relative's death. An evil omen was forecast: we have seen the colonial monster in his bathroom, naked, playing 'Mantindane', playing with his penis and anus. In consequence he was enraged. He caught us and dragged us to Makana Island, and there we were his prisoners. A curse has fallen on us. He is like the mole because he cannot see. He gropes in the blind alley of the tragedy of history. Is it here that the answer to the huge question-mark is concealed?

To us, being on the Island felt like being seated on the crest of a mighty wave, and it felt as if it might subside under the sea and swallow us all. It is a jumble of shrubs and plantations. Its grass and fields have many thorns. Wherever anyone puts his unsandalled foot it treads on thorns. The soil is made chiefly of crushed sea-shells.

The road led us down to the village. We sometimes worked there in the yards of the houses, cleaning and weeding, but on that day we passed through the village, two by two. We walked carelessly, deliberately making a noise all the time. We entered a bush area, and left the footpath. We disturbed nesting guinea-fowl and sent them scurrying in all directions. We kicked the short bushy grass, hoping to find eggs. Our guard was doing the same thing. He was not a bad chap; we had tamed him down. Our destination was the northern shore, where we were to get stones from the old quarry and carry them back to the docks, situated to the east. We were known as the Island roamers, doing any piece of work there was. We called our span the Hodoshe span. Hodoshe was the name we gave our span warder. It is a Xhosa name for the big green fly that feasts on human faeces. Although he knew the nickname, he did not know its meaning.

As we travelled back we heard that strangled noise, all of a sudden blasting the silence of the Island. It was that thing warning ships that mist was forming rapidly. We had never got used to it. It let out the sickening low of a dying cow, lowing continually; and the echo would carry very far, all over the Island, until the air was over-charged with monotonous reverberations.

There are noises in the Island that snap a man's state of stupor, making him scuttle out of his brooding shell. First, there is the incessant yelling of the span warder. Then the growl of the seagulls that flew over us. As if announcing our doom, they encircled our area in great numbers, and repeatedly unloaded their bombs into our dishes as we sat eating in the yard. No matter how much we tried to take cover, we would finish eating with our jackets and heads besmirched with bird-dung. Then when we left they would immediately land to feast on the remains.

Muzi

We set out for our cells one evening after work. We queued up in front of Block C. Behind us in the eating-square a constellation of aluminium dishes glistened like stars reflected in a window. A colony of seagulls took their supper here and there from the remains, in a commotion of squeals and swooping, and flapping convicts picking up the dishes. In twos we marched into the cells while we were counted. A warder touched everyone's shoulder to make sure he had counted each man. The chief and other warders stood by.

As soon as we entered the cells the usual unaccountable excitement began. Already the washbasins were busy and the showers hissed. I unrolled my mat and reclined on it. Then the noise dropped stage by stage to a worried quietness. I looked at Mbali. His face was drawn and he was talking in loud whispers. A word had passed swiftly across the cells, leaving worried faces in its trail, until it reached me when Mutle told me, almost growling: 'Muzi is dead.'

I had already braced myself for a shock, but I had never thought it could be this. A hiccup attacked my throat. 'When . . . hic?' The question came of its own accord; I didn't want to ask it. 'How . . . hic . . . how did it happen? . . . hic.'

Order had settled in the cells. Even the showers became less noisy, and the wind which blew against the rafters sang softly through them.

'He died today. He hadn't been getting any treatment.'

'What? How was that?' I asked.

'Damn, you know the state of things here.'

'I know he went to the hospital with an acute appendicitis. Then . . .' I stopped. That was it. Muzi had been refused admittance into that prison hospital on three occasions. The doctor declared

44

him too lazy to work. Understandable when you considered the huge and seemingly healthy body of Muzi. And when he was seriously ill, three days before his death, the doctor who came once a week to the Island had not yet come. 'The chief of the hospital suspects it was the rupture of that thing,' Mutle said, 'Gosh and gosh, how could it not have been known?'

'It was known,' another next to us put in. A number of listeners leaned over us. 'The doctor said it was rubbish when Muzi told him. He had it when he was outside prison, he told the doctor.'

'Curse that doctor.' I scowled.

'You know them, why are you surprised at them?' Mutle said.

'They are pigs,' someone said. 'Dogs,' another added.

'It wasn't bad when he was outside,' the other man said coolly, 'but the pig's food we eat here was certainly not good for him. It made it worse.'

Twilight was stealing away outside. A sombre dullness of light came into the cell. When I looked round, almost everyone was lying flat on his mat.

This memory compels a man to drag up more bitter pictures. Oom Joe, panting like a horse during a 'carry-on'. These carry-ons, as I have described before, were frequent. But this was a fatal one. Oom Joe comes along panting like a horse. Exhaustion defeated his efforts to outrun the blows. This was when the fiendish warders had a nice game. Two of them waited for crawling Oom Joe to come by and pass on. The prisoners ran to form a circle within the zinc prison and scores of warders lined up with batons in hand. Weary Oom Joe, coming lame behind the others, changed to a walking run. He couldn't help it. Two warders rushed at him. 'Come, run, run, lazy Poqo.' They lashed out. He twisted like a worm pierced by a nail. They were not delivering hard blows on the head. This was a new instruction, because in one of the previous 'carry-ons' they had closed the eyes of three prisoners. They had had to be taken to Cape Town for treatment. But then they diverted all their energy to the body. The result: Oom Joe sank down with crushed ribs.

45

'Stand up, bloody kaffir. Why are you sleeping?'

Oom Joe could not stand up or lift a leg. The mindless warders lashed on. The colonel gave a command. A chief warder shouted: 'Stop there.' When they stopped, a bloody, maimed Oom Joe was all that was left. He died later in Cape Town hospital.

The terror of this makes me stop.

The death of Muzi coincided with the release of Bekimpi from solitary confinement. This gave us such a shock that I nearly forgot about the death of Muzi. It could not be explained why they released him from there, but certainly it was after the visit of some prison big-shots. He was placed in our cell, C3. I met him with restrained eagerness.

'Jail is a place that changes a man,' he said when I asked him about Chi, the moment we settled down to chat. 'If you are not a sissy, if you are a toughy, that is, on a criminal offence, don't hope you will get out when your term expires. So be happy that you are in for a political offence.'

I listened, wondering where he was getting to.

'That is the plight of the common African prisoner,' he went on. 'A jailbird might start in on you, and if you turn to bash his jaws you invite a further charge. A raw criminal wants to compel you to a homosexual act. You lift up your hand in desperation and commit murder. You'll never see the outside again. But if you are a sissy the chances are high. So it is, in the police torture chambers. But let's leave Chi alone . . .'

Bekimpi was changed. He had grown thin and raw-skinned. He looked at me with blazing eyes, and I dared not start a longer conversation just yet. What was coming that night was a mourning gathering for the departed Muzi. This was to take place in all the cells. Bekimpi was to be the main speaker in our cell, and the chairman of the cell announced him.

'We should be having a welcome-gathering for Bekimpi here, but that's a happy occasion, and it can't be done with our sick hearts. We shall shelve it till next week,' the chairman said. The cell had become grave, like a graveyard gathering. The electric light shone on the face of Bekimpi standing at one end, and his face became sour like that of a man entering a mortuary.

46

He began in the voice I knew well, a power-punch baritone:

Island,
Have you claimed more victims?
You have.
Have you drowned more victims
In a fog more dense than laundry steam?
You have.

Sons of Africa,
Who fell by Attila's own grinding-axe,
Your death has not been causeless.
Like all of us, you were faced with a choice:
To live a slave-life
Or to live a free life.

Choice is a capacity by which
A man acts as his own defender
Or his own destroyer.
No one can escape the necessity of choice,
In any situation—action or inaction—
That confronts him.

You are compelled to choose
What you don't want—you scream;
Circumstances are unfavourable—you scream;
It's nature's way and you can't help it—you scream;
It's the despots around you
Imposing their will on you—you scream;

But, son of Africa,
You can always rebel.
I know you won't let
Irrationality cling on you like an oyster on a rock;
You won't live with irrationality like a dog lives with fleas.
That is your motivation to rebel;
That is your reason to reject the slave-life.

47

This is a necessity you can't escape:
Either a free life
Or a slave-life.
But a being that drags its body
Within the doldrums of serfdom
Is not to be envied.

No man has a right to subject you
To cheap labour,
To inferior education;
To curtail your movement
In the land of your birth;
To impose influx control on you,
To subject you to job-reservation,
To impose taxes upon you without representation,
To refuse you votes to choose your despots;
No one has a right to arrest the development of your mind,
To refuse you free expression
Because of the colour of your skin,
In your own motherland,
Being the fellow-producer of its civilisation.

The thick walls that encaged you,
The roof under which you died,
Tell of the fate of Makana.
In the thick mist and fog of the place,
Does not the spirit of Makana roam?
We don't know your place beyond the road you've travelled.
It is futile for us to claim
That your reward is somewhere beyond the grave,
Or that it's left to posterity to acquire.

Where are you, Simon Khuboni?
The piercing pain still lingering in your bulging eyes,
And the look of mockery in the face of the warder
Who saw you on your death-bed?
Where are you, Mountain Langbon,

With buckling knees under the weight of a wheelbarrow,
Terror flushing in your face, reflecting the wrath of the white
man?
Where are you, Pahle?
The ravenous seagulls predicting evil omen
Made the place smell like death.

Like idlers we shall eat
Of the fruits of your blood.
Like opportunists we shall pluck it, like looters.
But rest assured
Your names shall not dry from our lips.
Immortality has become a platitude,
A consolation of no value to you;
Yet we shall remember.

A military cap appeared at the little window in the passage. The figure of Bekimpi stood silhouetted against the light-struck yellow wall. Someone started a chant. We followed with a reverberating full-throatedness. Someone stood up and walked to the standing warder and said something to him. The warder walked away.

Later the man told us: 'I told the warder that we were having a church service for the dead Muzi.'

'So Chi broke down,' I said, looking at Bekimpi. He lay in a heap next to me, and our talk had come round to it, one evening. The winter rain throbbed painfully on the roof. Bekimpi's body twitched in answer to my question. The cold had beaten him pale black. Cold did not agree with him. His eyes opened and shut, and opened and shut. He glared at the roof, a corrugated asbestos roof. The throbbing on the roof seemed to strike on the lens of his eyes.

'My wife has been refused permission to see me,' he said, changing the subject.

I forgot to mention that Bekimpi was a married man and had two children. But this new subject was also bitter. I could see pain in his eyes. His mouth twisted. I will not dwell on the plight of his family: they had known his absences from home for short-term imprisonment before this, a separation more bitter than death, since then

49

there is the cherished mystical belief that the loved one might be enjoying the comforts of heaven. Since his arrest by the Saracens when he was thrown into a cell with pass-campaigners he had become a frequent political arrestee.

A tiny body dumped itself between us, giggled, and said: 'Give me a smoke, chaps.'

I did not turn to see who it was. I knew it was Thabo, a life-termer and T.B. case. Of all the prisoners who filled the cells and roamed the Island, Thabo was the one who sucked pity out of me till my throat was drained. Sleeping in his corner, he was capable of emitting a cough so painful it scratched the chests of those who heard it. He had been in the T.B. cell a number of times and was cast out when the Boers thought he was getting better.

'What smoke?' Beki grumbled (we used to shorten his name), 'You're doing a staff job.'

'Staff job?' Thabo squealed, 'Where have you seen a staff job in prison?'

'Cleaning the yard, that's a staff job. You should be organising smokes for us.'

'You talk shit,' Thabo said, and giggled. He didn't do hard work because of his illness. He and Beki had been together in previous arrests, and indeed it was Thabo who had converted Beki to the political cause when they met during the pass-campaign arrests. And now Thabo was also on a life-term sentence. He was hard and scraggy, and no one could guess his age. He coughed.

'Stop it,' Beki said. 'Man, you will put T.B. into us.'

He coughed again.

'What's wrong with these Boers, putting a T.B. case with us?' Beki went on. 'They want us to be infected?'

'To hell with you,' Thabo said, rising. 'There's ndalafa being eaten over there.'

'Go and chew your T.B. with them,' I said. He sauntered down to Jimmy's place, unperturbed.

'That's a bloody damn intellectual, that one,' I said, looking at Thabo squatting down at Jimmy's place. I heard Jimmy's grumbling heavy voice. His ndalafa was under attack. Ndalafa was a special dish prepared by convicts working in the kitchen. They smuggled in our ration and made their own kind of stew. The result was under-rationing of the prison to a state of starvation. Many of our men hated to see anyone eating ndalafa because of this.

'Quite a brilliant man,' said Beki after some time. 'But there's one man I think he can't beat to it. Soli. That boy . . .'

'Hey, where is Soli now?' I said eagerly. 'What happened to him?'

'How do I know? In Zambia, Tanzania, America, England, China, only his own skull knows. Or in a guerrilla camp, perhaps.'

'When did he skip?'

'Three months after his release in 1962. That's a fellow. I will tell you about him tomorrow. It's too late now.'

The following night Beki told me about Soli.

Soli

The sky was unusually overcast (Beki said). A grim dark cloud raced menacingly in from the west. Everyone knew that that cloud was the rain-carrier. Then there was the stench of rain in the dank air. It began with a soft drizzle.

Under the roof, that sadly muttered its time-old complaint at the thrashing of the storm, three young men reposed. They were in one of the mass of matchbox houses, indistinguishable from one another from any distance. A brick box in the recesses of a black man's retreat, his laager that is always vulnerable to the might of white repression: the location.

A long finger of lightning cut across the western horizon, stretching to the north. At the wink of an eye it had flashed blindingly through the windows of every house. As Zipho jumped to pull the curtains, the thunder replied with a roar that rumbled in the nerves of a man, and the walls seemed to shake.

'Yes, the cancer of our time,' Zipho said, as he pulled the curtains close, and ducked from the unseen blows of the thunder. This had been their talk all evening. Soli lay on the sofa. Next to him the radiogram, a long varnished thing that looked like a coffin, was playing. He switched it off on account of the thunderstorm. He opened a tape-recorder and switched it on to play *Got my mojo working*, Jimmy Smith's hit.

I was a patient listener there (Beki said). The room—something lush, indeed. The end-product of à man's toil, exploited or not. The few that scrape a living from the huge pot of the capitalist stew, and from its leavings, by God's chance, come out with a few coins. How many do it? Is this not a factor that hampers the liberation struggle: the reluctant and reactionary black middle class?

52

'Yes. The cancer of our time,' Zipho said again, as he sat on the sofa. It felt comfortable under his buttocks.

'Fortunately, my brother is not reactionary,' Soli observed. A faint twitch of anger ripped across his forehead. His brother was a successful retail trader.

'That is not the main danger,' Zipho put in. 'Those people: time will cure them. The danger is the cancer.'

Soli had just arrived from a one-and-a-half-year stretch in prison for Poqo activities. Zipho, who had escaped arrest by God's mercy, had come to visit his old friend.

'I don't care a damn about the cancer anywhere outside Africa,' bellowed the hardened Soli, and suddenly the scar on his right cheek grimly showed, as if reacting to his outburst.

Zipho noticed it twitch, and he grimaced, as if the whole incident was reflected in his mind, and he saw it as clearly as if he had been present when that warder tore Soli's cheek with a wire whip.

Soli went on: 'What is white domination in South Africa? What is white supremacy, herrenvolkism? What is apartheid for? Racialism, white racialism, bastard white racialism. Why talk about the cancer in the other places, when it is in your kitchen, on your table, in your bed. Anyhow, for the sake of human justice I will give it a moment's consideration, or even more.'

'Remember international racialism rides on the horse of imperialism,' Zipho said. 'I wonder why people should be more scared of bodily cancer, when racial cancer is more dangerous. Needless to count how many lives it is claiming in America. All over the world it is destroying lives, under cover of the thick dust of the imperialists' exploits. Racial tension is now rising in Britain.' He turned over the mass of papers and cuttings that lay on the table and the floor.

'Did you say racial tension is now starting up in Britain?' Soli asked. 'That had escaped me. But remember that even their Oxford Dictionary names us kaffirs. It does not even explain the meaning of that word. They can't deny that they attach a derogatory, or insulting, meaning to the word, no matter how they hide it. However, it doesn't hurt us, because we can call them something too.'

'Go on, I'm listening,' Zipho said, and shifted to make himself more comfortable on the sofa.

53

'Didn't you know that the virus is comfortably nestling in the blood of this old colonial bull? It was there since the beginning of the colonial era, or perhaps before. It was transported to this so-called new world, and throughout the world the zebra colours of colonial occupation have splashed the map with racial dung. The U.S.A. has markedly different racial groups; the disease spread like an epidemic and took root. In Britain it could not show, because there were no distinct racial groups. But now the Indians are flying in like swarming bees—huh.' After a pause he continued: 'Why should I regard the Scots, Welsh, Irish and English as different racial groups? In such a recognition the virus thrives. I would rather call them the tribes of Britain.'

He pulled his lower lip, and blew at the lamp; the incandescent flame glowed in his face.

'So you speak of races, and yet somehow you refuse to recognise their existence,' Zipho observed.

'In a manner of speaking I would recognise their existence. The word race was originally conceived to tell one group of people from another, just like a pastoral farmer differentiates between the cows: Jersey, Frisian, Shire, Africander. But as a whole they are all cows, whether brown or black, or white, or spotted, or coloured.'

'Oh, the cancer of our time!' Zipho exploded. Lightning flashed in the room. He threw himself on the carpet. 'Damn you, lightning. Why, it looks like it's in league with the racialists.'

The odour of roasted steak suddenly filled the room, so quickly, like a bottle of ether opened in the air, as Soli's sister-in-law came into the sitting room with tea. Soli's stomach grumbled, it grumbled aloud, and his brother, from the kitchen, called: 'What stray dove is that in the sitting room?'

'I don't like your political discussions,' Linda said, as she put the tray on the small table. Her face showed that she was in earnest. 'You think it was nice when you were away, Soli?' She fixed him with a penetrating gaze. Soli returned it with a loving smile and said nothing. She continued: 'Who suffered when the Boers took you away? Your friends or us?'

Her questions were rhetorical, and she left the room without waiting for an answer. She had carried herself with ease across the room,

54

and when Soli raised his eyes again, the elegant figure had disappeared into the kitchen.

Her voice reverberated from the kitchen.

'They're at it again—politics, politics,' she protested to her husband.

'That's too bad,' came his reply, and then silence.

It was frightfully dark now. The rain was falling even heavier. But in the room there was comfort. The tape-recorder was now playing Brooke Benton's *Lie to me*, the whole L.P. The music intermingled with the splutter on the roof, and became one with the melody of the rain, the murmuring of the distant thunder, and the rustling of the wind through the leaves of the peach and apricot trees that surrounded the house.

'Just as Nkrumah said,' Zipho put in. The spectre of black power is descending on the world like a thunder-cloud. Emerging from the ghettoes, swamps and cottonfields of America, it now haunts the streets, the legislative assemblies and the high councils. It has so shocked and horrified Americans that it is only now that they are beginning to grasp its full significance, and the fact that black America is also in confrontation with imperialism, exploitation and aggression in other parts of the world.

'I wonder if the idea of black power has any justification,' he went on. 'It tends to add pressure to the already tense racial situation. I always had fears that the Negroes might call down on themselves barbaric retaliation from the whites who are in the majority there.'

Soli drew a deep breath again: 'Has white power any justification? They have been dominating the world with the stranglehold of a giant lizard, assuming the role of Herrenvolk, right up to today. The Negro can't help it; he has been rejected throughout the world, throughout the centuries. The audacity and insolence of the white racialists are beyond man's comprehension. The Negro did not go willingly to America. He was ripped from Africa by force and made a slave; and today, in this twentieth century, he is rejected and spurned by the white, as if so much damage had not already been done to his whole being. The white owes him much: in blood and life. Yet he pays him back with a boot in the arse. All along, the Negro has been begging to be accepted as a human being, to be recognised as

55

such. He was not begging to sleep with white women, but to share in the wealth of America, of which he is a producer too. He has been rejected—scornfully rejected. Luther King is an instance of that begging. The new men reject begging. Do you think you can kick me out of your house, kick me out twice, and expect me to come back again? All along, the black race had been prepared to forgo their racial prejudice, primarily because they were the underdogs. They accepted integration, they have been begging for that, they demonstrated for that, they rioted for that. The white racial group rejected these advances. They rejected the black man with gun in hand. The whites have vested interests in the status quo—power, wealth, privilege and superiority. Then who is the more dangerous racialist?'

'Both,' Zipho said firmly.

Soli went on: 'The policy of integration demands that the Negro must beg to be integrated; and the white must be begged to accept the Negro. The whole concept of integration consists of persuading the poor lamb to make friends with the growling hyena. The hyena that regards the lamb as nothing else but the provider of its food, without which its survival is threatened. That is why the Black Muslims thrive. In Africa the basis of this concept has been changed by the death of colonialism. The lamb has suddenly acquired more power than the hyena, and doesn't have to beg for friendship. The hyena has had its teeth drawn and its claws pulled out, and now its growl is no more dangerous than the howl of a puppy. It has learned to live no more on the blood and flesh of the lamb, but to cultivate the soil and produce food. This is the fair base for integration when the parties concerned are the lamb and the hyena.'

Little Jabu came into the sitting room and sat next to his uncle.

'Jabu, come back here! I don't want you listening to that rot,' his mother called out from the kitchen. The thirteen-year-old boy slowly walked out of the room. Soli smiled wickedly. Then suddenly he remembered how tears had fallen unrestrained from the eyes of his sister-in-law, the last time he was convicted; how she had sobbed aloud when he was pushed down the dock. She had never deserted him throughout the time he was awaiting trial, and she had often travelled from the Reef to Pretoria where the case was heard. Each time she brought him food when he was in custody, a suppressed tear fell. And she looked very pretty when she wept. The sentences of ten to twenty years and life imprisonment imposed on other Poqos shocked her away from any involvement in politics. That was in 1962. She had always liked Soli, even before she married his brother; he had been her messenger at the time when her love-affair was still clandestine.

Soli had always stayed with his brother in the Reef. His parents and family remained in the Vaal. His sister-in-law was constantly worried about his health; he was tiny and a weakling. She was sure he would not last in jail. Even now, as he sat talking to Zipho, he was the picture of leanness, a cause of constant worry. It looked as if toil in the jail had sapped the last good tissue from his scraggy muscles. She could not blame Zipho for Soli's involvement in politics; it seemed rather that Soli had led Zipho. As soon as Soli was arrested, Zipho had disappeared, only appearing a year later with the story that he had been sick, and had been to see a witch-doctor in the Eastern Transvaal.

'Many armchair politicians, and the worst cynics of our time, have condemned the African nationalists as racialists. Granted, some are, but it is not without cause,' Soli said, starting the argument up again. 'One wonders whether it is possible, as someone once said, to hate the whip instead of the hand that wields the whip. In our case, the hand is that of the white voter, the white policeman and the white soldier. When the African nationalist reacts against this, the racial feeling is born in him. Yet what do they want an African leader to do, not to be considered a racialist? He must be either a puppet of the West or a communist.'

'But it's true,' Zipho said, 'that there's much prejudice among African, Coloured and Asian people. Though I think it is mostly the result of the political set-up, it thrives on inherent prejudices.'

'Yes,' Soli said. 'The relationship here is not that of the hyena and the lamb.'

'But you accuse the English more than you accuse the Germans. Don't forget that they murdered millions of Jews.'

'I don't exonerate the Germans,' Soli said. 'You must remember that a mad racialist was ruling Germany. The barbaric pogroms against the Jews in Tsarist Russia, Poland and other European states

57

show that any racialist despot mad enough to emulate Hitler would have murdered Jews in any of these countries like the Nazis. The operating force was just madness—ultra-insanity. But in Britain, as Segal says, it is only racialism at home that is recent. Only a society that believed itself to be racially superior could have run the slave trade for so long, or ruled a coloured empire with such confidence. They believed Britain had everything to teach and nothing to learn; and so they believed that they, the British, were naturally superior to those they ruled. A superiority confirmed by the distinction of colour . . . and again as Segal says, the British have always resented foreigners, though this never stopped them from going to settle in other people's countries.'

'I think I must agree with you there,' Zipho said, 'when the British are debarring black immigrants from the Commonwealth.'

'And remember,' Soli added, 'white immigrants, because they are white, are granted unrestricted entry into Britain. But get me clear on this: the Congolese may slaughter the Congolese, the Indonesians the Indonesians, and the Indians the Pakistanis; but here the fundamental danger is reduced, because prejudice, here, is not tainted with imperialism and Herrenvolkism. It's the struggle for political power that divides these people into factions of tribal or geographical origin. And unscrupulous politicians have exploited these divisions.'

There was a pause, and then Soli went on: 'Racialism is a mental disease. No amount of legislation or force can change a racial mind. The mind has been indoctrinated since childhood. There are many examples of this kind of teaching in our country. The children are taught from the cradle that we are kaffirs, monkeys—inferior beings. You know yourself. I worked in a white man's garden. The only . . .'

'Then you think the racialists must be allowed to wolf the whole country, unrestrained by law?' Zipho was leaping up in indignation.

'Not in such a hurry, my friend,' Soli waved him to sit down. 'The hope of mankind is counter-education from childhood. Do you understand me? Not what is being done today, where parents may object to mixed schools. It must be enforced by law, and with the use of soldiers if necessary. There must be legislation to thwart the reactionaries, to protect this way of combating racialism. There must be civil rights laws . . . but this will not be the end of the

58

struggle. Such steps will at first only make the racialists more bitter. You may succeed with political rights, legal rights or religious rights, but you won't see social integration or economic equality. You can legislate for a Meredith to go to an all-white university, but that will not make him acceptable to the rest of the students. They will make an island of him. Even in the buses in Swaziland, one can see a white among Africans who has withdrawn into himself, isolating himself. So we shall always see segregation within integration. Our hope lies in a long-term programme. Perhaps in a generation or two we might succeed, or this state of things may last for generations to come. The present generation consists of incorrigibles. Our hope is in this, that they will all die, and become extinct. We must make sure that the virus is buried with them.'

After a long pause I asked:

'Where is this Zipho now?'

'Only his own skull knows,' Beki said, indifferently.

Just then the bell rang. The shrill noise of it sounded in my ear-drums as if it was right inside me.

'It is time,' said Beki. Turning to face the other way, he bent his knees and pulled up the blanket, shrinking into it so that the huge man was now a shrunken heap.

'Tomorrow is another day,' said my neighbour on the other side. He jumped out of his blankets and ran to the toilet. There was movement up and down the cell.

'The bell has rung, gentlemen, please,' said the cell chief, clapping his hands to make us quiet. Military boots were heard, thumping along outside.

'Another day gone, gentlemen,' Jab said from his place.

'Shut up your big head,' someone said.

'It's full of brains!' Jab shouted.

'Johnny, Johnny, give me a smoke, man,' Dantshi said.

'Gentlemen, you're making a noise,' said the cell chief.

The lights clicked off. The warder passed to the next cell. There was shushing from all corners.

I stood up and went to the toilet. In the urinal there was a queue; I went and sat on the bucket.

Makana University

'Boo! Boo! Boo!'

'What's that? What's that?' someone asked, the question most of us wanted to ask.

'Boo! Boo! Boo!' went the strange voice. We listened, fascinated. It seemed to be near, yet it seemed to be far. It seemed to echo from the west, then in the same instant from the east. It vibrated in the air, then came flat along the ground, crawling through the grass.

'It's a windmill,' someone guessed.

'What kind of windmill boos?' another threw in.

It continued to boo, pausing for a time and then going on again.

'I heard that thing when we were at the Cape docks. Doesn't anyone remember?'

'Yes, I remember,' someone said; and then everyone remembered. But at that time it had been very faint.

'It must be that thing that warns ships of mist,' one ventured. This guess was supported by many. But as someone said, what should we chaps born far inland know about the sea and the ships, and things that went boo?

My first cell on the Island was C3. Immediately we arrived, two convicts were placed in charge of the cell. They spoke the 'district six' language of Cape Town, a variety of Afrikaans. Their behaviour and talk showed that they had lived often among Africans in Cape Town. Ari was the stouter and tougher one, the handsome one. We regarded him as the bodyguard of the other one. He was light-complexioned, with playful eyes. He was round. Almost every part of his body was round. He had a roundish head with a flat back to it. He had small circular ears, and a small spherical nose, and round plump buttocks.

The other one I so hated I even forget his name. He was a telling contrast to Ari: lean and raw, but hard. He had drawn features which told of his long years in prison, and thuggery was spelt out glaringly on his face, so that you might be inclined to agree with that Italian professor who said that incorrigible criminals are distinguishable by their features. His feet were crippled; they had permanently assumed, perhaps from childhood, the shape of a woman's high-heeled shoe. He was aggressive, arrogant and short-tempered.

Ari was the friendly and happy one. Jail never seemed to be a place of suffering for him. Early in the morning he would sing his favourite song, or his own version of it: 'Why does the sun keep on shining? Why does my heart keep on beating? Don't they know it is the end of the world? It ended when you said goodbye.' He would sing in a loud, full voice that echoed from the walls of the whole block, or go into a high-pitched, small voice that cracked on the rafters of the building like a whip-lash.

He worked around the prison, doing all sorts of nice odd jobs; and he would often come at weekends, when we were locked in, to sing at our door, holding on to the bars like a caged gorilla. It soon became clear that his singing was a calculated attempt to woo some of us like girls. He could not have done anything more likely to provoke our wrath against him, than to see not men, but prospective mistresses among us. He would sing the national songs with us and claim to be a criminal Poqo, in order to be near us.

Finally we came to a breach with him. At that time, other incorrigibles were sneaking into our cell, with the connivance of the authorities, who demanded in return a spy service from these criminals.

One day a young man from Randfontein skipped from our cell without anyone replacing him. He went to another cell for the weekend. On counting us up that evening, the warders found that one was missing from our cell. Ari immediately took it upon himself to hunt for the missing man all over the prison. With eyes wide open like an owl's, betraying the favour he anticipated from the warders, he soft-footed it into each cell, hunched, like the sniffing dog they used to hunt an escaped convict, with a mixture of fear and triumph on his face.

It often happened that a prisoner left his cell on a visit to another.

If he was not replaced by another in the cell he had left, the warders would search the whole prison for him, as if a Mafia thug was loose and the F.B.I. were hot on his trail. In most cases the prisoner would be watching the hunters, standing among the other prisoners in full view, like a grain of Epsom salt in a packet of sugar. In the cell to which our young man had gone, there was no increase in the number, because someone had gone to the spare-diet that day. If he had not been betrayed, the warders would have assumed that someone from our cell had gone to the spare-diet, as they often did. But Ari found him; and he was punished, with a brutal beating.

From that day on we ostracised Ari. He had to keep close to the door, where the other convicts gathered, out of fear of us.

Then it happened, not long after that incident, after knock-off time. He came into the cell at a fast, business-like pace, and pointed his long, trembling finger at a selected four. 'You . . . you . . . you . . .' moving fast from one to the other, as we sat some way apart from each other. 'You are wanted at the office,' he breathed fast as he spoke. The bitter line of his lower lip told how he had prepared a disastrous 'bomb' for us. At the door stood a young warder, waiting to escort us. We marched swiftly out of the cell. Boo! Boo! Boo! went the gnawing wail, as we marched to the offices. Its echo spread like a plastic lamina, sailing through the air, shining like liquid, and finally dissolving in the frightening dullness of the environment.

At the office we were confronted with the preposterous charge that we had held meetings where we planned to dynamite and burn the jail and kill all the warders. The chief warder smiled in disbelief. But in order not to discourage his spy ring, he removed us from the cell. I was sent to A4, the others to different cells in the various blocks. Bekimpi was not affected by this 'bomb' of C3. We were not surprised. He was too grave of countenance to tempt any trouble-monger. He had looked at Ari with eyes as stern as a savage's, and Ari had to pass him by.

Allegations of this sort were often, and astonishingly, taken seriously by the warders. The spy ring of convicts would add sometimes a ludicrous touch of alarm, as on the occasion when they told the authorities, with a note of apparent honesty, that all was ready; that we awaited the arrival of a ship from Mozambique loaded with arms,

62

and that they had heard us talking about this. The balance of probabilities was alarming, since at that time guerrilla insurrection in Mozambique was in the news. We did not go to work that day; the whole jail. We were securely locked in, and vigilant sentries with FN rifles took up positions round the prison. Many walked around in a menacing fashion, with hard, drawn, worried faces. The rest of the warders went to do military exercises. Naval guns boomed out two or three times. We saw new faces; reinforcements had been brought in from the mainland. There was a tension like when a rat is cornered by ten cats. The tension was so acute the cats could not get through it, any more than a bewildered fly trying to pass through a window pane.

We could not only feel fear, we seemed to see it, pegged out in space, swinging like a pendulum. The Boo! Boo! Boo! had an ominous tone. And the seagulls, as if they had heard a call to arms, circled the prison like Mirage fighters. But anyway we got a free holiday, as we always did on such days.

Changes in the precarious state of politics in the world were always reflected on the faces of the warders. A fiery speech at the U.N. or a resolution against South Africa echoed in ear-deafening thunder through gaping human maws, but transmitted into an expression of the opposite feeling: 'Kaffirs! Baboons!' And it showed itself in action; those with quick arms let them swing, and boots flew, always finding their target: the loins of a man, thudding on them like the sound of a huge bug falling from the ceiling on to the cement floor. And they made us work like mules. A statement by the O.A.U., or a successful guerrilla warfare operation near South Africa, triggered off worse reactions; the warders became as dangerous as cornered scorpions.

But such events as the fall of Ben Bella in a coup d'état, and the coming of U.D.I. in Rhodesia, were received with ecstatic joy. The fall of Nkrumah, too; we heard the news in 1966 that he had been overthrown by a coup in Ghana while he was on a visit to Peking. It was Saturday afternoon when we got the news. All of a sudden a cloud fell over the prison, a dark, grim cloud. It became dark in the daytime. A cool breeze that seemed to be pumped out of a refrigerator swept through the prison. Soon we were all shivering lumps of

63

flesh, wrapped in blankets, lying flat on our mats. The gloom was deeply felt, as if someone dear to us had passed away, the kind of gloom that pervades a family that has lost a beloved mother. We were witnessing the agony not of a family but of a nation, of the whole of Africa. It seemed ironic that Nkrumah was not dead; we felt that he was. We knew that the forces of imperialism had found a new foothold, having already been among us too long. Africa was open to free plundering, and its leaders were divided.

'Never before has a body so disjointed as O.A.U. made such an eloquent claim to unity,' said Thami of D4, who walked on crutches.

'Shut up, you lame thing. Long live O.A.U.!' said our demagogue, Lindi.

'Never before did unity make such a mocking irony of itself as in O.A.U.,' Thami said again, showing his broad teeth in an inspired grin.

'Shut up. Cowardly Boers, how can they bring a man on crutches here? Could this thing make a guerrilla fighter?'

'Shut your maw, cockroach. I'll beat you with this stick.' Thami advanced, hopping, lifting one of his crutches.

'If you come near me, I'll take the stick and beat you with it,' Lindi said, retreating. Thami went on, with the stick lifted. Lindi caught it in the air. Thami balanced on the crutch, held in Lindi's hands.

'O shame,' Viki said, advancing. 'Shame on you, dog . . . to beat an invalid with his own crutch.'

'Leave him alone. I'll break his skull,' Thami said, fire blazing in his eyes.

'The Boers did it,' Lindi said. 'They beat an invalid with his own crutches by bringing him here.'

Viki seized Lindi's foot and lifted it up high.

'Wait, wait,' Lindi shouted. 'Thami's balancing on the stick. He'll fall when I fall.'

'You're even. Each with one foot on the ground. Fight!' Vicki shouted.

Lindi fell. Thami fell hard on top of him.

'O.K., O.K.,' Lindi said from under Thami. 'Nkrumah is gone. Africa sails the stormy seas without a pilot, without a compass.'

64

Thami put his lame knee on Lindi's stomach and pressed down.

'And what happened when Balewa went? Eh, what happened?'

'We had the same disaster. Even today Nigeria is afflicted by that accursed deed.'

'Now you're a man again,' Thami said, lifting himself up, and laughing.

We read the politics of the world from the faces of the warders. The expressions on their faces were our news commentary on the way things were going in the outside world. Widening wrinkles in fits of anger, or smiles of triumph; red, glaring eyes and louder mouths when faced with setbacks, or drawling self-flattery when they were happy about something. So went our news commentary. But not all the warders knew anything about the shifting sands of world politics. It was the top warders who read the newspapers and passed on their moods to their juniors. Receiving such news at second-hand, in a distorted form, these warders became either angry hyenas or circus clowns.

In my new cell A4, I dumped myself down between a hefty guy from Johannesburg and the mathematician Nzobo from Gemtown. This cell was in charge of a considerate criminal who, we thought would not give us the same kind of trouble as Ari.

In A4 I gave up trying to obtain permission to study. My lectures were stuck in the receiving office, in my kit. My brother at home was paying the Damelin college for a dead horse. I had begun studying under Damelin when I was at Kroonstad, but at the Island we had to re-apply for permission to study, and I was ignored. So I went dancing, swinging my legs in ungraceful steps. Nzobo, besides being a mathematician, was good at dancing, and gave us lessons, together with a light-complexioned, bespectacled young man from the Cape. I had begun to learn dancing in Leeukop, and went on with it at Kroonstad, going about it coolly. Now in A4 I went about it violently: fox-trotting, jump-jumping in the quickstep, and going sluggishly up and down in the waltz, and jerking my knees dangerously in the violent tango. But it never worked out, and today I am just as good as if I had never started with it.

Christmas of 1964 sneaked up on us prisoners while I was in A4.

We were determined to feel like human beings. Believers in Christ and non-believers, we all participated in the feasting of 1964 to celebrate the birth of Christ. We organised a community chest. The warders agreed that we should each buy one Rand's worth of biscuits and sweets, and fifty cents' worth of toilet things. We pooled our stuff for the sake of those who did not have any money to buy anything. Ah, those assorted biscuits—the crunchy roughness of the ginger cream, the dissolving roughness of the Marie, the crackling smoothness of the lemon cream, and the soft coarseness of the wafers! Everyone had a share, P.A.C. men and A.N.C. men, who were mixed in about the same proportions in all the cells, by chance rather than intention; in the whole jail the P.A.C. men were in the majority.

In our times off, concerts and shows were staged. The Islanders, a combo group from A4, gave us a hell of an entertainment. There was Bra Bob, the tycoon of Port Elizabeth, the greatest Master of Ceremonies the Island had ever had, leading the Islanders in a blasting crescendo of sweet music. He spoke the words of the song, *Lakushona ilanga* (*At sunset*) and the choir sang it beautifully, sending me off on a voyage of nostalgia. I was not a show fan outside, I did not have time to attend concerts; but the Islanders broke up my peace, the complacency with which I had accepted my lot, with this piercing nostalgia, the longing . . . longing . . .

It was not the first time that we had had concerts in prison. We had them in Pretoria, in Leeukop and Kroonstad. But on this day it brought on that longing; we really missed the outside.

In jail I had suddenly become a socialite, so they said, teasing me. A friend would ask me: 'Which one are you today, Danny, the socialite or the socialist?' Dancing defeated me, but I really believed I could sing, judging from the applause and cheering of the audience. So I went at it full-throated in concerts, stretching my vocal cords to snapping point in what I thought was sweet music. It was not until I sang into a tape-recorder at home and played it back that I realised what a donkey-voice I brayed in, crude and rude and untutored.

From classical and soul music we changed to location gumbagumba. We twisted our intestines in jive twist, and patted our bodies until they were sore in jive Phataphata and Shala jive. The Islanders blasted the horn for us: that is, they blew through their mouths, humming.

A few weeks after the New Year holiday I left A4 of my own free will and went to A2. I changed places with a fellow who was bored with his cell. The warders did not know who was sleeping where, except with a few who had been in so much trouble that even the warders knew their names. All they knew was the total number in each cell. They were like a man who has two dovecotes, and does not know which dove is in which cote.

I stayed in A2, lost in the sheath of black pigmentation behind which a warder could not identify an individual. Here I went full out on Judo lessons. I had tried Judo now and then since Pretoria, in Leeukop and in C3. Then I decided to take it on at A2. I staggered on with it. But the only thing I could do well was studying. So I decided to press again for permission, and after a stay of less than three months on the Island I got it. So I landed in C1, Makana University.

When I asked for permission, the head warder, Theron, said: 'What are you going to do with your studies?'

If I seriously wanted to study, I had to say 'Baas'. To avoid this, I spoke through an interpreter in Zulu. The interpreter was a political prisoner, a real tsotsi type.

'I want to study. I have been granted permission, eight months ago,' I said, looking only at the interpreter.

'I said what are you going to do with your studies?' he repeated, fixing me with a mocking eye. Asking favours from an enemy breaks one's spirit. I sensed that the whole business had political connotations.

'I just want to study, that's all,' I said coolly.

'Do you want to answer me or not?' he barked all of a sudden. I realised the game was lost. I had to wait for the next weekend. Then it was the same head warder, but he had forgotten me, since there were many who asked for the same thing. And he was in a good mood. He stood patting his right leg with his swagger stick. He was a hefty, big-buttocked man, with deep-set eyes, deep set because of his jutting forehead. He was cruel and thorough. Cruel to all: convicts, warders and us. Thorough in the sense that within the regulations he pressed hard; without the regulations, he did not. And he had the patience to listen to complaints, though not of granting them always. He was somehow preferable to the other head warders and colonels.

He had a way of disappointing his warders. One day after work a warder nicknamed Makwarini (after the quarry) pushed a prisoner ignominiously into Theron's office.

'What do you want?' the head warder barked.

In a quivering voice, Makwarini said: 'Chief, this damn . . .'

'Don't talk of damns in my office,' snapped the chief. In jail, Afrikaans has become an insulting language. Every sentence must have a bad word in it, even when the warders are talking together, and not about us. They are used to it.

'Chief,' he began again, not knowing what had annoyed his superior, 'Chief, this prisoner calls me Makwarini.' He was trembling.

'What is your name?' The chief's voice seemed to crack the ceiling.

'Snyman, Chief.' Makwarini was trembling more than ever.

'What do you want, wasting my time? Go!'

Without a word, Makwarini led his prisoner out and let him go, humiliated.

It is surprising how much the warders were afraid of their superiors. I don't know whether it was discipline. But they were sometimes annoyed when we did not show any sign of fear of their chiefs and colonels. We just looked them straight in their eyes. Since the inflow of the political prisoners into the jails, the authorities had been confronted with a new subject: self-disciplined, cool, not begging, not cringing, not crouching, not expecting favours, but always complaining and claiming his rights within the regulations. For the first time, copies of the regulations were given to the prisoners, studies were allowed, libraries had to be opened—and yet, oh, ingratitude! Before the advent of this type of prisoner, the warder was dealing with convicts: servile, ignorant, selling each other for favours, full of fear, every man for himself. Now they were confronted with united men, taking concerted actions like hunger-strikes, men who would never give witness against a brother who had committed any kind of offence in jail.

I was finally at the university. I pushed in with a boy from home, to share a desk with him. The desk was one of a long line of desks, a single piece of furniture, exactly like school desks. It was attached to the wall below the window-line, stretching from one end of the room to the other. It was divided into compartments. I assimilated myself into C1 like a shooting-star dissolving in the darkness of the night. Soon I was taking a part in staging a mock trial, and again in staging a mock parliament. C1 was the cooking-pot of cultural activity. Our souls were enriched, uplifted from the eroded substratum of basic living. When we staged *Animal Farm*, man, we did not care what military-cap peeped through the window, and did not give a damn for his barking, meal-stop or no meal-stop. And we did not think of infringement of copyright. It was enriching the soul, just as when we staged *Back in your Backyard* in Leeukop.

When your soul is low, sunk to the level of brainwashing through dejection, depression, frustration and despair, that is when the white man gets you. Soon you become a stooge, a pimp, a traitor to your cause. At a vague mention of remission that would land you back at home, you immediately sell a friend. But when the Summitones or the Islanders come to C1 to compete against our cell group, then you witness things. And that is enriching the soul.

The winter of 1965 gently stole in as early as March, and then more aggressively in April and May, stampeding the cowardly autumn out of the Island. At times the timid sun would be bold enough to send a tiny ray of hope through the thick blanket of rain-soaked clouds. But the winter rains, yes, they were the Island. The bloom of beauty was rapidly waning, leaving a desolate land, a soil of crushed sea-shells.

We instituted rapid changes in our cell to retain the summer warmth. Sleeping-blocks were established; four men sleeping on three mats. The fourth mat was used as a pillow. The cell, once crowded from one end to the other, now seemed half empty as we stretched out on the mats crowded into a lesser space.

We were counted one day after work. Then we dug into serious studies. Soon it started to get dark. Military boots stepped into the passage to click the lights on. This was a moment for relaxation. Light talk started from corners. The mats were already spread.

'Gentlemen, it is still study-time, please,' our study-chief reminded us. We elected the study-chief from among ourselves once a month.

69

He also took charge of the cell; we ignored the convict supposed to be administering it.

Then it grew dark outside, and the murmuring became louder. Soon most threw their books away and started talking freely. At this stage our study-chief could not control us. Some spoke of their plans, others discussed plays and debates; the gymnasts began their practice in the toilet; our cell combo began learning new songs, also in the toilet; and some youths recalled their love exploits at home, in sharply nostalgic tale-telling.

The murmur rose to a general noise, until the bell rang the hour for sleep. Yet we continued talking. 'Gentlemen, the bell has gone, please,' our cell-chief pleaded. We were silent for a moment, then started again. Military boots stepped hard, coming to switch the lights off, yelling at the same time: 'You're making a noise there! Silence!'

We went dead. But stubborn whispering started up in the corners once more, as soon as the warder had left. Our study-chief did his best to silence us. There were some responsible men who fell silent as soon as it was time. But for some of us it was difficult; to cut our talk in mid-sentence, in the darkness that settled down like a fallen ceiling. We had to finish such sentences. The whole subject could not be left hanging over until the following day, and a man could not leave out a certain point in an argument he was winning.

It was a long time before silence fell on the whole prison. I went really dead. Then my eyes were forced open. The cell was brightly lit. Could it be morning? Then I was aware of military-caps behind the door. The door rattled in terror as the clank of keys forced it open.

'Fall in!' barked a warder in a high-pitched voice. Why fall in at this time of night? Before we could stand up, they were inside, in full force. I could not count them; they were many.

'Face the wall!' came another order.

'Leave the damn rags,' barked another one, as some of us tried to dress. We clung to the wall, naked, like statues on the Voortrekker monument.

'Don't look back!' another barked at us, and the windows rattled. Knock . . . knock . . . some mischievous little warder was provoking our hatred by knocking at our heads with a stick while we looked at

70

the wall. Somehow I realised that he was stealing these hits on us, making sure that the captain did not see him.

Holding on to that wall reminded me of the finger pierced right into the anus when we were searched in Leeukop. There we had stood facing the wall. Then we bent over. Hands on the ground. Then a painful rough push in the anus, searching for anything that might be hidden in there. I dreaded this treatment like I dreaded the extraction of a tooth. It was true that criminals hid things in there. Fortunately, here we were spared the finger treatment. When they left, the cell looked ugly. Nothing less than a vandal could have passed there to mess the place up like that. Mats and blankets flung about, no one knew where. If we had not marked the blankets with initials, no one would have got back his own blanket. Those with old and dirty ones would try to keep better ones belonging to someone else. Still, we had to wait until the following morning to sort them out. They switched off the lights before we had finished making our beds. Our books were not much interfered with. One of us had glanced at the watch of a warder; it was about 2.00 a.m. We fell dead asleep once more, for an age.

The Kulukudu

Bekimpi went back to the kulukudu while I was still in A2 . . . The clank of knocking metal faintly registered in my sleeping mind. I must have been conditioned to react to it, because I was virtually asleep when that clank twitched the cord joining sleep to wakefulness.

'Shit,' was the first word that escaped my lips. I did not want to wake up so early, because it was Saturday. Why must sleep slip away from me at weekends, the time I most wanted it; only to come full strength on work days, to hold me fast in the blankets, unable to lift even an elbow, as if I were glued inside there? Those chaps in the kitchen were knocking the mugs and dishes together, disturbing the whole prison. Chris next to me was still snoring, a sound like rawhide hauled over rough ground; but most of us were fully awake. We tugged the stale blankets over our heads in a last attempt to summon sleep afresh.

The stale blankets, that were never washed, puffed a persistent, but mild, nauseating stench which, since my nostrils were now used to it, was accepted as part of the normal air-intake of my lungs. The air was heavy with the breath of unrinsed mouths and the sweat evaporating, thick and stale, mingling with the stench given off by the blankets. The dank air rose in a bid to escape but was arrested by the window-panes, and it settled there; there it thickened, painting the panes misty, the colour of coal-ash, looking as if someone had purposely breathed on them.

Usually I slept solidly—first stop morning—and was deaf and dumb to the biting of fleas and bugs. But as soon as I woke up I was aware of painful itches in certain parts of my body. No one spoke about the bugs, which were fortunately not too bad. But the sight of lice sent shivers through everyone.

72

Clank-clank, clink-clink went the mugs and dishes. 'Shit!' I cursed again. The stomach remembered food, in an ever-increasing hunger. They started working in the kitchen at about four. And I always woke at the same time, about five. At weekends it is good when one wakes up at seven. The pale twilight overwhelmed the large un-curtained windows, and expelled darkness inch by inch out of the cell. Everyone seemed still to be sleeping, there was not a sound of breathing, but a scratching of fleabites and muffled curses. Most of us slept facing the ceiling, raised knees making tents with the blankets. Heaps on both sides of the cell, leaving a passage in the middle, stretching towards the door. The mats were laid at right angles to the walls, but the bodies that lay there, heads to the wall, were at any angle to it: some curved and coiled, others knees up, and others facing downwards, flat, stomachs on the hard mats. Some of the heaps were so flat that you would not know there was a human being under the blanket, others huge as fallen tree-trunks.

Thud thud thud, the hard stepping of oncoming boots. Then click, and the cell went yellow with bright electric light. A pink face under a military cap peered through the small window. 'Damn him, what's wrong with the bum?' Curses escaped mouths in muffled tones. 'Has he forgotten it's Saturday?' Then the face left the window, and click, the light died in an instant. What was left was the light of a fresh dawn. 'That's right, shit.' The men were irritable this morning. But that was the general attitude: no compromise with the man who despises you. Gradually the half-light of the dawn was giving way to a brighter light. The sky was clear of clouds.

Then the bell cracked in a shrilling sound. Its intensity sickened the nerves. 'Izwe lethu!—The land is ours!' The shout cut through the still dark air of the cell, coming from a corner in a stirring greeting to us all. We responded with equal strength: 'I Afrika!' Yet we still lay in our blankets, some murmuring, others meditating. But the gym-nasts jumped out of the blankets and went to the toilet for their morning exercises. I thought of what I should do when I got out of bed: wash my shorts and my shirt and jacket, or swap them for washed ones. There is a special span that washes the clothes; and those who were lazy handed in their dirty ones for clean ones. But there was always the danger of receiving rags for your good ones.

73

And wearing clothes when you do not know who wore them the previous week is abominable. It was one good thing about the Island, that they let us wash our own clothes, though they lost their heads sometimes and ordered us to hand over our clothes for clean ones. But in most jails on the mainland no prisoner was allowed to wash his own clothes.

'Fak, I am not going to wash my clothes today,' someone whispered to his neighbour.

'What are you going to do? Change?'

'What the hell, no. I am going to leave them as they are. They are clean.'

'Don't kid yourself. You'll get meal-stop. Don't expect pity, you'll get none from me.'

Sunday was the day for inspection. The colonel, or whoever it might be, expected us to be clean, or it was meal-stop.

We lay on. Then we heard the thud-thud of many boots. Someone jumped to the window, and announced: 'Hei, fall in, ma-Afrika. Here come the Boers.' We jumped up, but already there was the clank of keys and the rattle of the door. Our cell was the first to be counted in this block.

'Fall in,' barked a military cap, as we fumbled to push the blankets aside, lest they tread on them. 'You still sleeping? Bastards! This isn't a hotel, or your mother's home.'

We struggled to form twos in the passage.

'You're out of order, damn you,' the warder scowled. 'You'll get meal-stop, you Poqos.' He had to start afresh, forgetting what he had counted because of his howling. Four warders counted: 'Shwt shwt shwt shwt . . .' the sound of silent counting escaped their lips. 'Shwt shwt sixty!' each one burst out immediately he finished, in triumph, as if he had solved the toughest problem in algebra. Sometimes wrong counting made them repeat it in all the cells.

They banged the door when they left. Some of us went back into our blankets, until there was a second rattling of the door and a bark of 'Fall in!', followed by swearing and threats of meal-stops when they saw we were still in our blankets. We went to take our morning dish of soft porridge and black coffee.

That was A2, about 7.30 in the morning. Military caps hung

74

around the entrance of each section. Usually it was C section that went to get food first. A line of two-twos stretched out like football fans lined up to witness Chincha Guluva at their local ground. All the prisoners in white jackets, without which one forfeited a dish. Aluminium mugs and dishes glistened in the fresh morning sun, reflecting a tar-shining glint on the dark faces; they felt a sense of being human beings. The warders resented it with a painful shrug of their shoulders. If we had grown a tail or horns they would have felt better.

I watched them pass, jackets buttoned, in neat lines. I watched them take their food, slowly, with a pronounced indifference. It was a sharp contrast to Leeukop prison; there we used to run as if a monstrous ghost was full speed at our heels, a distance of about 440 yards to the kitchen, to collect one lousy dish. We would reduce speed when we reached the kitchen, then, dashing past, snatch up a dish as a hawk swoops down in a fowl-run, and within an instant sails up into the sky with a chick in its claws. It required some skill, moving at such a speed, to pick the dish with the largest piece of pork. The dishes were laid out on a table which was just an extended window-sill, and inside the kitchen a convict was throwing dishes on that table, two at a time, as fast as he could. I remembered a friend, Vich, who was an expert at dish-grabbing. At a distance, while taking the curve towards the table, he had spotted the dish with the loveliest piece of pork, and—swip—he passed on with it . . .

Now we at A section had our turn to go to the kitchen. We sat eating in the cell. Soon we heard the song of the dishes, as the spoon scraped clean the soft porridge until the shining of the dish was reflected on the face of the man. The hour passed quickly. Soon we were busy with our attire, washing it clean. In all the sections, clothes hung on the opened windows like the insides of a cow at a butcher's.

Soon the lunch hour struck, at 11.00 a.m. Supper would be at about 3.00 p.m. The C section went for their hard-boiled mealies. We stood at our windows and looked on. The men were clad in blankets, wrapped like skirts round their loins, because they had washed their shorts. When they had turned from the kitchen with the dish and a mug of the white powdered maize beverage called puzamandla, and were

75

marching back towards the cell, a warder grabbed Bekimpi and yelled: 'Go back, with your blankets.'

Go back where? He was already coming back from the kitchen.

'But I have washed my shorts,' Bekimpi protested.

'To hell with your shorts. You know blankets are not allowed in the lines,' the warder said, grabbing him and pulling him out of the line.

'Am I the only one you see in blankets?' Beki asked quietly.

'Quiet!' the warder barked at him, and made a move to stop the rest.

'Look, it is not the first time we have worn blankets. We have . . .'

'Quiet, baboon,' the warder snapped, turning towards him.

Beki was a man whose reaction to things was unpredictable. Now the warder's eyes were boring into him, the eyes of baaskapism that caused the many with slave-minds to cringe. Beki's reaction was different. A fit of anger fermented in his stomach, compressed and exploded in a swing of the arm holding the puzamandla. The liquid splashed on the bewildered pink face; the military cap landed indecently on the dirty ground when the head was jerked back. The thick white liquid flowed like vomit down the military tunic.

The next moment Beki was whisked to the kulukudu. The Island was a place where a week could not pass without some breathtaking incident like this taking place. The kulukudu were little cells for spare-diet and solitary confinement. There were many of them, housed in a ghastly building adjoining the reception offices. Ghastly, that is, in its purpose and the way that purpose was carried out. But an ignorant tourist, observing it at a distance, would conclude that it was a nice building belonging to a rich private estate. The passages leading to the little cells were as clean as hospital floors–polished red. Some convict was doing a queer form of waltz, as he slid over the floor, shining it with the cloth under his feet. No direct rays of the sun shone in the passage. There was only a dim light inside there, like on a heavily overcast evening. Through the upper windows of the little cells, thin beams shining like rectangular laminae extended down to the floor, at acute angles with the wall when the sun was high in the sky; lowering, they picked out the angular figures of men stretched on the mats. These men were Mandela, Sisulu, Kathrada and the rest of the Rivonia group; and others who were on the starving list. The Rivonia group were all in solitary confinement, and Beki was too; but he was also placed on the starving list.

When I was in the spare-diet for three days, I saw these men having exercise in the big yard walled round by the cells. I did exercise there too, with the other spare-diets. Sometimes the Mandela group would work in that yard, breaking the slate-black stones small, and the small stones even smaller, like old Mashamat and the rest of them in the quarry. Then they left off working in the yard, and went to dig the lime sand where the Hodoshe span had once worked.

It is ghastly in solitary confinement; but men could stand it with dignity. I had stayed in solitary confinement while awaiting trial. Then, apprehension about my fate preoccupied my thoughts. But immediately after I was convicted I was confined alone again for a month. Overwhelmed by depression, I was offered a bible. I read it avidly; I drank of it like a starving calf sucking milk from its mother. In order not to come out a thorough Christian convert, I had to read it critically, trying to confute and contradict it. I brought it under the scrutiny of the mind, the basic tool of our survival, focusing it on the screen of scientific principles; though I knew that religion could not be judged in the same light as scientific phenomena, being a matter of faith only, and that I did not have to go to these lengths to answer it, but only to look at it in the light of the political set-up in South Africa. And to enjoy it fully, I asked for one written in Shangani. I liked the language. And I had to recognise a wealth of literature in this big book. Then once I also found in the prison library a historical novel set in the Roman Empire, which set the corpuscles of my blood circulating at cosmic speed . . .

But staying in the kulukudu alone, with hunger also to contend with, was something different. The walls of the cell looming as if they would tumble on you; the narrowness of the cell suffocating and pressing on you, so that you felt that the world had squeezed you into a corner; and with thoughts of frustration and despair to haunt you in nightmares, the blank walls with nothing hanging on them assuming the shape of monstrous creatures; and having nothing to do for months but eat and sleep, walk about and sit down, stand up again

77

and lie down, wash yourself and empty your stomach into the little bucket in the corner, only a small distance from your mat, within your eye range, so that you could see the dregs inside there, then you would feel like vomiting. This is what would happen if you were given to fits of mental depression. Then you would start playing your childhood games, but like a lunatic, because you were alone. You would play Apsikotshi or hopscotch in the square grooves of the cell floor. You would call out 'Emi, emi!' for 'I'm in!', and you would jump, calling out 'Jumpi, jumpi!' for 'Jumped in'. Then you would play marbles with the grains of your hard-boiled maize, throwing each one into your mouth when you felt like a bite. And you would play Ludo, throwing the dice alone. Then you would get bored and start singing, howling through the whole prison, until a night warder silenced you with a yell. Then you would watch the flies buzzing up and down like comets. You would wonder what the flies wanted in jail. But you would watch them still, chasing each other, then watch them mating and get amused. You know then that you are near breakdown. But if you are a strong man, you will stand it. I have seen a few men breaking, dismantling spiritually like a statue of sand when it gets dry, just crumbling.

Beki and the Mandela group were strong men. For punishment Beki received seven cuts, on the buttocks. He swallowed all the moans that tried to escape from his mouth.

Bekimpi is Visited

A strange figure in civilian clothes was seen in the corridor of the offices. Pointed moustaches, black as a cat's fur. Blue eyes flaring like the flame of an electric welder. Hefty shoulders. Inspector Van der Merwe had arrived.

Bekimpi stood in the colonel's office. The colonel sat on a chair behind a desk. The early morning sun came in in oblique rays, one of which fell on the colonel's face and magnified a pimple on the cheek. Bekimpi observed the pimple, red and growing, sprouting a cluster of tiny pimples all over the face. As the rays from the upper window slid down the line of the neck, Bekimpi observed the border of pimple lotion. The colonel raised his eyes. Bekimpi looked away. His eyes moved over the walls, blue-painted. Portraits hung there: conspicuous was one of Premier Verwoerd, and again one of Vorster. Engrossed in his observation of the room, spacious and lush, he did not notice a man coming in. A cat's footfalls in brown suede shoes. The usual shoes walking about here were boots announcing themselves, thud, thud.

'Good morning,' the colonel greeted him. Bekimpi didn't turn to look. The man approached and passed him. 'Good morning,' he said to the colonel. The man was not Van der Merwe, but a short, stout man. Bekimpi wondered how many of them there were. The man turned to look at Bekimpi.

'Ach, he doesn't look like a bad kaffir, colonel,' he said in Afrikaans.

'No, no, that's true. He isn't bad at all. It's not in his nature.'

'I see, colonel. It's just the bad company which he always keeps.'

'That's correct. I'll leave you alone to chat with this man. Where is Van der Merwe?'

79

'He's coming now. Good, colonel.'

The colonel walked out. Beki wanted to spit. He felt the actual spit full in his mouth, contempt thick in his throat. He knew a lot about this kind of talk, and how many men fell for it.

Van der Merwe walked in.

'Hello, Beki,' he said, with a comradely smile on his lips. Bekimpi was not surprised when he was greeted so intimately by a man he had never seen before. Even the warders would not shorten his name like that.

'I am not going to talk much with you today, Beki. But I want to give you time to think. You are here on a life sentence. I have arranged that you will be discharged any time you are ready to work with me. I hope you understand. Of course you do. No, no . . . don't worry about answering me now. I'll come back again. Do you smoke? Here.'

He offered Bekimpi a cigarette. Bekimpi refused it.

'Don't be afraid, you can get special permission to smoke if I arrange it. See that you tell the colonel, Du Plessis. Also, put some money for him in the office. He can buy soap and things he needs. That's in order. I am a bloody good man. You may take Beki back, Du Plessis.'

'Come,' Du Plessis said.

Bekimpi walked first. He could hear Van der Merwe going on: 'It is useless for a man to rot here when there is a way out. I am a very kind man.'

Back in the little cell, Bekimpi walked up and down, taking short steps from wall to wall. He laughed. He nearly kicked the little bucket, turned and laughed again. He wanted to laugh hard, but he knew that he had been insulted. Then he felt the pain of the insult. He stopped pacing. He tried to laugh, but coughed up a groan. The pain came as convulsive stabs to the heart. 'Do they think I'm a woman?' He felt eager for revenge. He knew how he was going to be revenged. He was going to disappoint them. That would be his revenge. He wanted them to come to him again. Then he became impatient. The rattle of the grille farther down the passage made his heart beat faster. Every time footsteps approached his cell he thought it was them. He felt angry, cold and sour.

The sun raced over the cell. Dishes clanked farther away. His stomach was hungry. The man next door got his food: half-boiled maize grains and liquid puzamandla. The food tray came to his door. Bread and fat and black coffee was placed before him. The convict didn't look at him. Nor the warder with the convict. He looked at them both, and his hand stretched out to take another dish with maize grains.

'Take this one here,' the convict said.

'You're making a mistake. This food is for Coloureds,' Bekimpi said.

'Ach, take it, man,' the warder said, almost shouting. It looked as if he was angry that this kaffir was to get the ration for Coloureds and Indians; as if he had not been told why.

'A lucky mistake,' Bekimpi said to himself, and took the food. He ate it with a good appetite. It was only when he had finished that he thought more about it. He remembered the special-branch police. This was a trick of theirs. 'Let me see what supper will be. It may have been a mistake. But this was supper ration for the Indians: another mistake. I should have got mealie-rice, for lunch.' He was in a mood to talk to himself.

Food for supper was bread and fat and coffee. He refused it. The warder ordered it to be placed inside the cell, and they locked the door.

The following morning it was bread and fat and coffee again. The warder looked at the previous night's food, still untouched.

'Why didn't you eat it?'

'I'm not eating this either,' Bekimpi said. 'Give me my right food.'

'You're bloody mad. It's your stomach. I don't care.' The warder stormed out, leaving the fresh food too.

Bekimpi felt very hungry. 'So this is their game?' He felt hardened; his stomach hurt. His eyes looked gluttonously at the uneaten food, now four rations.

With the fifth ration Van der Merwe came. He poked his nose into the cell, smiling. 'Hello, Beki . . .' He stopped, seeing the hard look on Bekimpi's face. 'Why have you not eaten?' he asked, like a father asking his son.

81

'This is not food for kaffir prisoners,' Beki said, bitterly.

The inspector shouted at the warders: 'Give him the food he wants. Is this how you treat a man here?' He walked out.

Bekimpi felt as if he was breaking. He had won, but he felt dispirited. Solitary confinement . . . He was asleep: he was dreaming . . .

Bekimpi's Dream: Zweli

His eyes opened. He glared at the roof: a corrugated asbestos roof. For a moment his mind was blank. A feeling of insecurity; and then his mind was crammed with heavy thoughts. He remembered he had had a night of ghastly dreams. He tried to recall them, but was interrupted by a shouted slogan. Someone shouted it from a corner of the cell. The whole cell responded with a yell that reverberated through the whole building, with a deafening sound.

A white warder appeared at the window. His face was expressionless. It showed only the indignation of a man who had worked a night shift against his will. It was 5.00 a.m., a promising Friday morning. The sky was clear of clouds. The warder barked once, and walked away from the window with a sleepy gait. The sound encouraged the feeling that it would be a fine day, because the warder's anger was mild.

Beki was lying on his back, blinking at the roof. His muscles were tense, though they were used to the hard floor of the cell, and the hard mat he was sleeping on. He turned his head, and his neck was cricked. This did not worry him; his neck was used to the hard pillow fashioned by rolling the grass mat. He turned to sleep on his side. A friend was lying next to him, staring at him. He seemed to be able to read his mind: it was clouded with thoughts, fretting in their intensity. This was Thabo, and he was Zweli. Thabo and he, Zweli, had been friends for a long time now. They first got acquainted in jail, and they had stayed together ever since. Their transfer from one jail to another always found them in the same list. Now the separation that was on hand came as a blow to Thabo. For many days past he had tried to prepare a cushion for it, but when the hour came the cushion proved to be too thin and soft to weaken the impact. He,

83

Thabo, was left with a lifetime of prison sentence, and his friend was to be discharged. Thabo was a T.B. case, but was recovering fast; he had been discharged from the prison hospital.

Bekimpi returned to himself briefly. There was a man of the third cell, his namesake, who was indeed to be discharged. That man was named Zweli, and Bekimpi was pretending that he was the other Zweli. He liked to think that way. It was a good way of thinking. To be Zweli was good; to be going home was good.

He thought of Van der Merwe and his promise. Van der Merwe was an honest man. Bekimpi went back to playing Zweli, and like Zweli he was lying with us all in the cells, listening to Thabo. It was not a true dream now, but a deliberate act of the imagination. His mind felt glad to hear Thabo speak; he felt pity for Thabo. His mind was with us in the cell; only his body remained in the kulukudu.

Thabo's eyes were piercing. He avoided meeting them. And now Thabo spoke: 'Zweli, my brother, do not interpret what I am going to say now otherwise than in the way I mean it. Since you know me.'

He went on:

Our past is empty and it has no beginning;
Our future is blurred and it has no destination.
Go home and eat, go home and enjoy yourself.
Marry and beget offspring and be happy.
But in here I am doomed for life.
My people have forsaken me; our forebears have forsaken me.
Our misery lies in the fact that we have no base for our morale,
    and for our dedication.
Our base hitherto is our weakness; it is our complex.
We float in the air; we have no legacy.
We do not know the beauty of our land, because of
    misinterpreted histories;
We have never seen it as beautiful.
All we know is that it is full of smog and sinkholes, and the
    ground below us is hollow.
They have blamed it on erosion and on ignorance.

84

The grass has turned yellow and burnt;
They have blamed it on rainless seasons.
Fare thee well, brother, and rediscover yourself;
Discover your past; discover your base . . .
For there lies our survival.

Zweli cringed inside his blanket, and looked blankly past Thabo. A voice rescued him with a shout: 'Kuyahanjwa!' This means 'We are going'; and it referred to him, Zweli, who was going home. He had been in jail now for more than three years.

He lay still and closed his eyes, so that he would not see the face of Thabo. Everything that had passed through his mind when he was in solitary confinement, doing a 21-day spell of spare-diet, came back to him again; including the castles he had built in the skies, the fanciful thinking, the fretting. All these came back to him, vividly. That is the gruesome purpose of solitary confinement: to break a man completely, both morally and mentally. It is a kind of brain-washing. If a man wants to brood undisturbed, that is the place for it. If he wants to give himself up to meditation, that is the place for it. But it is also the place, whether you want it to be or not, for negative thinking: for fretting, self-pity, regret, and a crushing weight of remorse. You feel that the world has rejected you; relatives and friends, all have rejected you. Whatever attention your family and friends can give you, you feel it is not enough. You feel forsaken and forlorn, and finally you give in to melancholia.

That was the state of Zweli during those days. He felt there was a vacuum somewhere in himself that must be filled. On his fifteenth day a pattern of emotional development had taken place. Self-pity had given way to wishing the best for himself, and this in turn to castle-building. This led on to meditation, a meditation that sought a subject and a goal.

'There she stands, though indiscernible, in the shadows of my imagination. I am a man, and must marry. I must find myself the right woman. Soon I will be released. I will go home . . .' His imagination began to play. 'Ah, there she is: I can see her, though she appears dimly. Surely she cannot be Thandi? But who is she?'

He was talking to himself, like a madman. The vacuum was

beginning to be filled, though by what he could not say. He felt a change from negative thinking to positive thinking; during the following days he felt much better.

The mythical woman appeared frequently in his imagination. Every day a fresh quality was added to this woman, until she became a Helen of his heart, with the highest physical and mental endowments. He formed various pictures of her, giving her different qualities. Not one of his past lovers had come up to this standard, not even Thandi. But it was disheartening that this girl did not live on earth, but in his imagination.

He tried to define the limits of the territory he had to discover. 'She is an African, a city lady, young and beautiful, educated, intelligent, faithful, honest and well-behaved, charming and modest yet not shy, lively and gay, slender and attractive, very clean and smart . . .'

'Ha! Ha, hell!' he yelled, in his thoughts, as his concentration was distracted by a fly that whizzed past his face. 'This is a mockery of my imagination, and it is insulting to my intelligence. Where on earth could I find such a girl?'

He dismissed the whole idea and tried to form a more modest one. But every time he pictured a simple girl, she too automatically grew wonderful attributes. When he rejected her, the next would begin by being quite a simple girl, and turn rapidly into the most fantastic woman he could imagine. He felt cheated. He roared: 'This is what solitary confinement does to a man. It cheats him of his proper reason and his rational judgment.' Yet it had been an interesting fable; a good experience for someone who had only himself to speak to, who had only his own imagination to use as a book, who had hunger to contend with, and who had nothing to do the whole day but to sit, sleep or walk around in the kulukudu.

Thabo shook him. He came back from dreamland. He felt that same sense of insecurity again. When he opened his eyes, Thabo was looking at him. He closed them again, and went back to meditating.

With an effort, he recollected what he had seen during the night, in his dream:

They all stood naked, facing the wall. There were about fifty of them. A white warder moved from one to the next. He had a bowl of soapy water, and wore a thin leather glove on his right hand.

'Maximum!' an African convict shouted. His face spelt trouble. He was a hardened jailbird. He bowed in servility when he passed the warder, grinning and cringing like a dog wagging its tail before its master. Zweli watched the warder coming nearer and nearer. Every one that the warder passed jumped forward in a reflex action that made him hit against the wall he was facing.

As the warder approached, each man had to touch the ground with his fingers and remain in that bending position. Then the warder thrust his finger through the anus. When it came to Zweli's turn, the thrust was so painful that he woke from his dream. The pain seemed to linger on even after he woke; but he remembered that maximum security prison, with the guards walking with their FN rifles along a walkway attached to the roofs.

He was Bekimpi, in solitary confinement. Somewhere was a friendly Van der Merwe, and somewhere a Zweli who was leaving prison at the expiry of his term, all making up the confused mind of Bekimpi. But these same pleasant thoughts came to him every moment he allowed himself to think them. So he continued to imagine himself to be Zweli, in the cell with Thabo and the rest of us. And we sang a goodbye to him.

He dozed off, and the dream started again: Zweli's dream. He heard the roar of motor-car engines. Two trucks were negotiating a bend, on a sharp climb. They changed into second gear, with a squeak that would have frightened a drunkard sober. He was in one of those trucks. It was a prison draft to a new jail. They arrived at one in the morning. It was so dark he could hardly see his finger. The reception got busy immediately they arrived. A white officer sat on the chair, writing at a table. A reception convict, an old-timer, a shrewd black fellow, who looked younger than his age, moved up and down, talking as he did so.

'John Khumalo, your worship. Five-six-two, your worship. A pair of brown eyes, your worship, long ears, no scar, no marks; a belt, a watch and no money, your worship; a pair of trousers, a pair of shoes, a pair of socks, a shirt, a jacket, and that's all, your worship.'

The convict continued to detail the property of each prisoner, with the speed of a market salesman on a busy buying morning, performing his job like an automatic machine. Zweli wondered at this queer person. His admiration of the convict's efficiency was so great that he ceased to pay attention to anything else. Smack!—a rough dry hand collided with his cheek. 'Wake up, stop day-dreaming!' the convict yelled. This actually woke him up, breaking into the dream.

He lay still and was aware of Thabo next to him. But why did he dream in a pattern that followed the real story of Zweli's imprisonment? For the rest of the night, notable incidents that had happened in the past months came back to him: and the agony of being a man in chains, the agony of his arrest and of the brutal treatment that all of them suffered.

Sun-rays shot through the window, and from a distance he could see warders. The door was jerked open.

'Fall in!' a white warder yelled at the top of his voice.

It was checking time. The prisoners sprang out of their beds and lined up. The counting started. It was done by five warders, headed by a fat, big-bellied warder with deepset eyes that glowed with hatred. He had a stick, a symbol of rank. He used it for counting, poking each man as he passed: he was a head warder.

Everything was quiet after the checking. Zweli went back to his bed. He lay still. After what seemed like half a century, he saw two men standing at the door with their cups in their hands. Then one prisoner after another went to the door and stood there. Soon the whole cell was lined up at the door. He remembered that he had heard a faint clink of cups in the kitchen, a hint that food was coming. He pondered over this matter. Hunger had made his fellow-men like Pavlov's experimental dogs. He was no longer affected by it, because that day he would be a free man. He had simply lost his appetite; though he was still hungry.

When food was at last brought in, he also joined the line. His dish was overflowing with soft porridge, with a touch of sugar in the centre. His cup was full of a soup made from bean powder. This time it was a little thicker than usual, fresh milk being the standard of thickness. While he was drinking the soup, five men were queuing up for a share out of his dish. He did not feel like eating this soft porridge, so he gave them the dish. After barely a couple of minutes, the song of empty dishes started, spoons scraping their sides.

88

At that moment, the old bum yelled again: 'Fall in!' The door was jerked open. The prisoners scurried to the yard and lined up in their own spans. There were seven cells altogether, with a yard in the middle. The largest span had an indefinite number of men. Here there was always a marked disorder to be seen: a reluctance of the prisoners to fall into lines, and a continuous reverse shifting, no one wanting to be in the front line or even in the first thirty from the front line. But it was all done with the cunning of convicts, to baffle the eyes of the warders, so that they might not realise the extent of the disorder. Each prisoner sought to avoid the tragedy of having to toil in the vine-fields. In that span of about fifty, the thirty unlucky ones from the front were to go to work, and the twenty lucky ones from the back were to remain behind.

Zweli did not go to work that day, because it was his last day. Jerking his head to the right, he saw another single line of men queuing up by a cell that had been converted into a hospital. Inside slept men who were suffering from T.B., asthma and skin diseases. Those with minor complaints, or what the doctor regarded as minor complaints, had to queue every morning for treatment and then go to work. The doctor was from the local village. The next to be treated was a bow-legged man, his head too big for the size of his body; deepset large eyes and protruding cheekbones. He pointed to his neck; the doctor could see nothing wrong. The hospital warder caught hold of the sleeve of his jacket and pulled him out of the line, to go and follow the big span. The poor man merely grinned and walked away. Zweli thought of the tricks some of the prisoners used in order to avoid work. He stared at the man walking off; he looked like a duck waddling on dry land.

He turned back towards the cell. Four men were seated on the buckets. This bald statement hardly gives a clear picture of what it was actually like to see them sitting there: the cell was a bedroom, dining room, sitting room and lavatory, all in one. The men sat there as if they were relieving themselves, but it was all pretence. Immediately he entered the cell they asked him eagerly: 'Are they gone?'

'Yes,' he said.

All of them happily stood up. The foul smell started up from the buckets after them, filling the whole cell with a suffocating odour.

He did not hurry out; his nose was used to such smells. Neither did he retreat from the advancing army of flies coming from the buckets.

This was the way some men beat the 'fall-in'.

He spent the whole day thinking over his life behind the bars; its excitements, its grief and its happy hours. He thought with admiration of the stoicism and resignation of his brothers. The time moved fast: soon the spans came in to lunch, to fill their empty bellies this time with Gaboom mealies. What had happened to his dish in the morning happened again. He felt strong compassion for his brothers. When the time came near for him to leave, a fellow-prisoner asked him to make a hurried change of clothes; this was the only way to obtain a decent pair of trousers without having to appeal to the highest officials.

The hour came at last. He looked at himself in his civilian clothes; he felt very uncomfortable in them. His shoes made him walk with a limp, feeling very tall. For many months he had walked barefoot in the vineyards.

The gate was opened for him. He hesitated. His feet seemed to make a backward movement. He knew that he was free; nothing could dispute the fact, but his emotions could not accept it.

Once out, he jumped forward, and glanced sideways, unable to believe that he was really out. Here was that feeling of insecurity again . . . He inhaled a cupful of air and set off, followed by the echoes of the slogans of the brothers he was leaving behind.

Bekimpi's Dream: Thandi

His eyes opened; he glared at the roof. A corrugated asbestos roof. For a moment his mind was blank. Then, moving slightly, he pressed his elbow on to the bed; it seemed to sink into it. He started. He looked around. 'Ah, I am at home . . .'

He had had a wonderful sleep. What annoyed him was that he still dreamed he was in jail. He was welcome at home; there was a lot of excitement, a show of great happiness. His mother received him with tears of joy. To her, he was like a prodigal son. A white hen was offered to him, and slain, as a thanksgiving to the gods.

The morning was fine. Peeping through the window, he saw a goat tied to a pole. So there would, after all, be a party, to welcome him home. It was not a shameful crime for which he had been sentenced. He had murdered no one, stolen nobody's property; he had done nothing to offend anyone, So he was welcome. A ceremony was planned. He did not view with cynicism those who worshipped many gods instead of one, or worshipped the ancestors as well as practising Christianity. He did not condemn or shun his family's ancestral rites, even when they involved him in them; he knew they had no bearing on him and his conscience need not be troubled. He himself was still trying to formulate tenable ideas on religion, God, the meaning of creation. He could not accept Christianity for political and scientific reasons, and at school he had been looked on as a rebel against religion; but now he had sobered down. He knew that religion was a matter of faith, not of reason.

He remembered his doves. He got up, dressed and went out.

Willie sat on a brick, watching the doves. He was a small boy, nearly three years old. He had not been born when Zweli went to prison. He was the son of Maria, who had been a young girl then. Zweli, looking at the child, remembered how he himself had often

91

sat there, watching the doves. A male dove saw a female one on the ground. It flew down and started the art of love-making, sweeping the floor with its spread tail, in a graceful movement calculated to win the admiration of the female, all the time cooing in a rhythmical pattern that made a reverberating crescendo of sound. Doves are always experts in love-making. In no time the female yielded. Zweli thought: 'Female doves are not cheap females; they are hard to break.' The mating was violently interrupted by another dove, which appeared to be the lawful partner of the female. Doves are like human beings: they have an instinct to possess each other. There was a lashing of wings; surely this was a grave adultery, which might culminate in the divorce court.

The boy was elated. Zweli turned to go. As he neared the door, Willie screamed: 'Zweli!' The cat had entered the dove-cot; all this time it had been watching from behind the bricks. So, the monster never misses an opportunity, Zweli thought. Willie had already thwarted its intentions. Zweli let fly a stone, but it went wild and landed on a hen nearby. The hen squawked and jumped to one side. This only reminded the cock next to it that it was its mating time. It grabbed the hen by the neck and outraged it.

Before Zweli could intercept the cat, it had disappeared behind a corner. Just then a flock of doves flew in, encircled the house and landed gracefully on the roof. A neighbour's young girl could be heard shouting: 'Thirty for love!' So there were thirty doves . . . he admired the girl's rapid counting, but wondered if she had the number right.

'It's nice to be home,' he thought. He was feeling better. He went back happily into the house. His sister Maria had prepared warm water, and the kettle was boiling. He took his time over washing himself.

'Here is Thandi,' Maria called out, in some excitement. Thandi came in at a hurried pace, as if the wind was lifting her off the ground. Her flushed face showed her impatience as she looked around the kitchen. The door to the other rooms was shut, so she could not see where Zweli was. Maria's face was full of smiles, her eyes questioning.

'Where is he?' Thandi asked.

'How did you know he was here?' Maria asked happily.

'Did you think there is anything you can hide nowadays? Besides, I have been counting the days.'

Zweli recognised that voice, and did not know whether to be happy or not. This girl had stood by him up to the last hour, and here she was again, just as he was beginning a new life. They had been in love since he was at school, and it was believed that she had remained loyal to him while he was in jail. His family loved her, and she was a friend of his sister's.

He finished washing. He did not want to appear too soon; 'this damn girl . . .' he thought, going no further with the reflection. Yet he had an urge to see this woman. Before he had made any conscious decision, he found himself in the kitchen.

'Hello, Thandi,' he said, restraining his excitement.

She blushed, stood up, looked down and said nothing. There were conflicting emotions showing on her face: a conspicuous attempt to conceal her joy; a desire to burst into tears; an urge to throw herself into his arms. He offered her his hand. She took it. He felt hot, and for a time could not think properly. He looked around; his mother was not there, only his sister. He decided to defy convention, and touched her lips with his. She blushed and said nothing. Kissing is a sacred thing among Africans. There was a pause. Then:

'Sakubona makoti: good morning, my daughter-in-law,' a voice said from behind him. His mother had just entered. Zweli took the opportunity of disappearing behind the door. He was sweating; he needed time to think.

From time to time Bekimpi pulled his mind back to his own surroundings. Then he would wonder why he was thinking of these girls, instead of his wife. At times it amused him to play at being Zweli; at others, it annoyed him terribly. But it did not seem to be any longer a matter for him to decide; he could not help it.

'What is happening to me?' Zweli asked himself. 'I can't understand my own feelings. Perhaps I am being unkind to this girl; perhaps I am a fool. Do I love her or not? Why ask myself such a question? Love has defied the attempts of many a poet and

93

philosopher to define it. Yet when I was in jail I decided I did not want her any more. I felt there was something lacking in her which I needed.

'But why must my parents love this girl? What do they see in her which I do not see?

'Of course, I know: old people judge a woman by her diligence: whether she is lazy or not. They judge the extent of her respect for older people, her moral conduct, her loyalty to her husband. But I, Zweli, want more than that.

'True, by the definition of older people Thandi makes the grade. She was loyal to me, and I received no vulgar reports about her such as I heard about Zondile and Thembi. Possibly my informers gave me a biased report. But no; I am doing the girl an injustice. I knew her from school; she was not the cheating type.

'Her loyalty shows sound moral principles, honesty and love, since without these there can be no loyalty. Thandi is foremost in these qualities among all my girls; they are what grown-up people like in her; and, to be frank, they are what men like in a woman. Her busy hands are a fact too. Elders close their eyes to beauty; they do not care whether a bride is ugly or plain, smart or not. As long as she can work she is all right. Yet I cannot deny that Thandi is beautiful. Even more so when she is angry: very beautiful.

'Then what more do I want? I am asking more than any poor girl could give.'

He reached for a suitcase and fished out a photograph. There she stood, elegant and sparkling. She had sent this photo to him when he was in jail. It had provided a support for him in his gloomiest hours, that at least there was someone in the form of a woman who cared for him.

Thandi was an intelligent girl, who had done well at school. He got out a letter from the case, the only one he had decided to reply to. He read it again:

Dear Zweli,

I hold you dearer than anyone else on earth, even relatives and parents, because the life of a woman ultimately requires her to relinquish bonds with her parents to merge with a loved one throughout her lifetime. Here the special role of parent ceases, and her life is entirely linked with his.

But this cruel, unwarranted separation has dug a hole that will not be filled as long as you are away from me. It is a source of unspoken grief; it has left me with unbearable pains. Every day I pray for your safety and happiness, though you are in a place that has no affinity with happiness. I know your strength and courage; so that even where you are you are certainly not shedding tears, but are triumphing; it is only us who are crying for you, but we cannot help ourselves, feeling this way. I will wait for you, Zweli, no matter what happens. I love you, I will be faithful to you.

Yours lovingly,
Thandi.

'Could this be the girl I am looking for? My imaginary lady? But no: I dismissed her with all the others. Then what is this stupid uncertainty? The fault does not lie with Thandi; it lies with me. I have become fanciful. I have always sought to be rational, and instead I have become irrational. Who is this girl in my mind? Who is this damn bitch who is pestering me?'

He had become emotional; this outburst sounded to him quite loud. He was frightened that those in the kitchen might have overheard everything. Yet the outburst had been in his mind alone, and not in spoken words.

That evening the goat was killed. Relatives and friends gathered. Blood was sprinkled on the family altar. Ancestors were mentioned by name, those whose names were known at all, and their praises were sung. He watched all this with amusement. He saw his cousin George presiding over things. He liked to see that cousin bustling about, especially in matters concerning the security of the family. George was much older than himself.

George . . . the face of Thandi turned into the face of Bekimpi's wife. Now his imagination was playing tricks with him. He was seeing Thandi before they were married: and Thandi . . . Thandi was his wife's name. But his mind went back to George. He used to like George. George's presence stimulated feelings of responsibility, of

95

initiative. Zweli wondered how he would have managed, if he had been in George's boots. He could not even slay a fowl.

Immediately Grandma had finished addressing the spirits—she was the only one who had the authority to do it, and knew how—George made a big fire of wood, since it was a chilly night. He asked for benches to be brought for all the old men who lingered on in the yard in groups, all talking about the one thing: the return of the prodigal son. George also got himself a can of beer.

Zweli himself wandered off round a corner. But he chose the wrong corner: there ahead of him stood a group of girls, Thandi among them. He could not turn back, so he went on. He took the girl by the hand and led her into the darkness.

He felt very hungry and weak, and the place was stinking. A warder shot a beam of light into the little cell, and passed on. He had been in this filthy cell for six days now, eating nothing but dirty rice water. He remembered how he had clashed with the span warder. Twenty-one days spare-diet. Later there was the rattle of the door and the clank of keys. Warders burst in: 'Wake up! Stand up! Face the wall!' The angry warder yelled at the top of his voice. Naked he stood facing the wall. The place was ransacked; the place was left in an ugly state. The blankets were hurled into the corners. The mat had hit against the little bucket and spilled its contents over the entire floor, so that the whole cell was stinking. At the same time, someone was kicking the door of the next cell. His own door was closed with a bang that shook the whole building. It also shook him out of his sleep . . .

'Damn it, it is only a dream. I am still at home. But why must I keep dreaming about that damn place?'

He could not remember when he had parted with Thandi, but it must have been about 2.00 a.m. He thought about her: how she was now grown up, and had become a beautiful shape, not like before he went to jail. He was shivering; the dream had been bad. He felt insecure. He dozed off again.

Luminous rays of the sun shot into the room. He opened his eyes.

'Ah, this is good,' he thought. 'If only it hadn't been for that bad dream.'

96

'Zweli, I've been out.' Willie shot into the room.

'You've been out? Where did you go?'

'To the shop to buy bread. We went by car, with Kay. Zweli, why didn't you wake up and drive the car? It's nice. It says vrumm, vrumm.'

'Willie!' his mother called. 'Willie, come here!'

'I don't want to. Leave me alone!' the boy called back.

'Willie, Kay's going out in the car.'

The boy darted out of the room, banging the door as he went. Zweli heard him go out to the garage and come back again.

'It's not true. The car's still there.'

'Take this letter and give it to your uncle,' he heard the voice of his sister. Willie came in again.

'Zweli, here's your letter.'

Zweli wondered who it could be from; a letter delivered by hand, so early in the morning.

Dear Zweli,

    In the first place, I want to say how glad I am you are back, and to ask how you are. We are still living. Forgive me for not writing even a short letter when you were still in jail, but it is not my fault, no one would give me your address . . .

Here the letter switched to Zulu. Zweli angrily interrupted his reading. 'This damn Zulu bores me. Why doesn't she finish it in English since she started it that way, even though she thinks in Zulu while she writes in English? Who is this wench, anyway?' He turned over the pages of the letter and came to the end:

Your loving
Joyce.

'So that's the woman. She knew all about sex, as much as a girl in a brothel. She was very good at it. I remember getting a letter that mentioned how she was carrying on . . .'

He read through the letter. After the Zulu part, the end was in English again:

'I hope you will remember me, like the old days. Zweli, I love you very much. Please come and dry my tears . . .'

97

He tossed the letter aside: 'This girl makes me laugh.'

He dressed and went to the kitchen. It was Sunday. His sister said: 'Church?' He mumbled something.

'You ought to go to church and thank God you're back,' she said. He eyed her wickedly and went out.

He was with Sipho and Shoni, friends of long standing, at Biza's home. They were playing Jimmy Smith and Johnny Hodges. *I got my mojo workin'*, played by Jimmy Smith, filled the sitting room with its soul-searching music. It created a sweet tension; everyone was elated. Smith's voice was hoarse but pleasing. Heads moved in rhythm with the music, feet tapped, everyone was shaking his body while still seated. Then Sipho and Biza stood up, responding zealously to the challenge of the music. They made similar steps, producing a co-ordinated and harmonious shaking of the limbs, to the blustering shower of sweet notes from the organ.

'What do you call this?' Zweli asked Shoni.

'It's Medicine Jive.' Jail had made Zweli archaic, years out of date. New jive styles and fashions had come and gone. He glanced through the window and saw a girl in tight-fitting red trousers. She was with two other girls; she leaned on the fence, moving her hips and her body in time with the mojo playing.

'Who's she?' he asked.

'That's Emma, my neighbour. Don't you know her? Thembi's sister.'

'Her, don't tell me it's my Thembi's sister. So grown up and cute.'

Sipho said: 'Don't be shocked. There are lots of them. Your old friends are now mothers with illegitimate babies. They're sluts.'

'I must correct you,' Zweli said. 'Don't call the daughters of Africa sluts, even if some of them are. Would you like your sister to be referred to like that? And calling the children illegitimate is an antiquated, Christian notion. Why should they suffer for the sins of their unmarried parents?'

A heated argument ensued. Glancing outside, he saw she was still there. He felt hungry and asked his friends to go home with him.

They passed through Kgasoane Street. A group of tsotsis was kneeling or crouching over the dice. There were several groups; they did not give way to passing vehicles. Some were standing at the street corner, leaning on the fences or the electricity poles; others were jiving in the shebeens. The blurting of Umbaqanga, a kind of African jive, could be heard at the end of the street, and the unrestrained shouts of girls: 'Isimanje-manje', another new jive style; the modern ways. People were always advised that the street was too dangerous to frequent.

There was Emma again, now in blue slacks. He could not understand the nature of his feelings towards this girl. She went into a shebeen and began dancing the Smodern jive; all at once everyone round about there was jiving Smodern.

'How wonderful,' Zweli said to his friends. 'Africans are a happy lot. They are mirthful, if any nation is. They laugh as if they had no sorrows; they revel as if they had no problems, and they eat as if what they ate was something good.'

A man was mishandling Emma, mauling her about. Instead of being annoyed, she broke away, giggling. That destroyed Zweli's feelings, now he had completely read the girl's character. Certainly she was not the girl he had in mind, but he wondered whether he could not do with some sexual enjoyment with her. It was obvious that she was following him.

The sound of sweet music reached his ears. He felt as if some girl, somewhere, was singing just for him. Then he shook his head: it was the FM programme, in full blast. He lay relaxed and listened. It was nice to be home. It was Maria's habit to play the FM programme early in the morning.

Now he was grown up, he thought: twenty-four. But his educational ambition was not fulfilled. He dreaded the idea of going back to school. He felt he would not see eye to eye with the teachers. He had been a trouble-maker in his earlier years, and now his spirit of rebellion was aggravated by his stay in prison. Now he abhorred any kind of supervision. His aim was to study for the senior certificate by correspondence, but this part-time studying meant he would have to work. And work meant supervision, working under orders. The fact was, he was afraid of work.

He would like to channel his ambitions towards a profession he could practise independently. Only in this way could he develop a rational mind. Being under supervision, he thought, would frustrate and handicap his energies and his initiative, those qualities so important to his capacity for reasoning. To be a factory worker was to be turned into a mechanical human being; such was the effect of specialisation. And he hated office routine, it was monotonous and boring.

'But no,'–he checked himself–'I cannot set out to change the world. There seems to be no alternative to the systems that are operating now. Specialisation, regardless of its side effects, remains the best system for obtaining higher productivity. People must work in order that we can eat, in order that a man can enjoy life with his ideal woman. Yet I cannot run away from the fact that I hate working under supervision. As a physician, a lawyer or a cobbler I would be serving society as well as my ability permits me. But the tragedy is that we cannot all be dentists; and this is the tragedy of all those who have to be factory-tools in the present set-up. And it is these men who would cry out about unemployment if the factory owners replaced them with uncomplaining robots. No, something drastic has to be done, but what?'

He paused in his thoughts, and the music from the radio, which he had heard only faintly while thinking, became louder than he had realised, as if someone had gone in to switch it to a higher volume. He fidgeted about on the bed, and the music changed to Benton's blues.

He remembered well how the previous day had passed, and the fight that had started in Kgasoane Street the moment they were safely out of it. A man had had to jump over fence after fence, holding up his trousers with one hand to prevent them from falling down about his knees. Two tsotsis were hot on his trail, one of them carrying a butcher's knife. Drunken girls looked on, shouting, while older men and women watched the incident with dismay. No one dared to help the poor bastard. He remembered that he had had a night of hair-raising dreams, and had felt nervous the whole night through. He tried to divert his thoughts: he thought about Emma; he made up his mind to sleep with her. He thought about Thandi; so far she was the best woman.

100

'So now it is Monday, and I am still in bed. This is bad. Other men have gone to work. But who says I am afraid of work? I have been working like the devil in jail. Besides, I have only arrived three days ago; no one expects me to be working so soon.'

No one had said he was afraid of work except his own conscience. He got up and walked about the yard, looking at the doves, with little Willie by his side, talking a lot. The sky was rapidly becoming darker. A cloud came sweeping from the east, a ghastly blanket that covered the entire sky. One drop after another, rain started to fall.

'It is raining,' he exclaimed, and ran towards the house; but near the door he stopped short. He felt a painful sting in his heart. The plight of his brothers in prison, especially Thabo, came back to his mind. They dared not run away from the rain, until the warder, who was under shelter, decided it was time they could take cover. Now his act of running away from the rain surprised him: since when had he been able to do that of his own accord?

'Perhaps it has to be so. These men are prisoners, and it is not to be expected that they will be treated like schoolchildren. But what about the free working man?'

The thought set his knees shaking. He must admit it, he was afraid of work. Then what would happen during the intervening years until he was an independent attorney or something like that, in a practice of his own? He was afraid even to think about it.

Whether he liked it or not, he had to work in the months that followed. But he was a reluctant working man. He could not get the clerical position he very much wanted, so he worked in a departmental store as a packer and general assistant.

Every day, after work, he had complaints. One day, it was an aching back, another, exhausted knees, and the next, an unbearable headache. And always fatigue. He went to a doctor, who told him he would be all right in a month's time. The aches persisted, and he went to another, who told him it was the strain of modern times; nothing could be done about it. 'Strain of modern times': he pondered about this idea when he was alone.

One day, when the shop was packed with customers, someone took his stamp by mistake. It was too much. 'If I find the person who took

101

my stamp, I'll bash his jaws,' he raved. The next day it was the manager: 'This blockhead of a manager is insane. How does he expect me to do this? He must know I've only two hands.'

Another day he missed his record-book.

'Who is this bum after me?' he boomed.

His cousin, with whom he worked, was a believer in witchcraft. He said: 'I told you, you have to be careful, or they'll fart your head off your neck. How did that cow-dung get into your locker? Answer me that one.'

He did not answer. He knew how it came to be there: biscuit-boxes that had been ordered had come in smeared with it. But he did not tell his cousin.

Later he found his record-book in the inside pocket of his jacket, and remembered putting it there himself. He kept his mouth shut about that too . . .

Bekimpi pulled himself together. He looked round at everything in his kulukudu; the blankets were bundled together and he had been sitting on them, gazing blankly into space. His lav bucket was in the corner, half full. The sun was moving slowly across the floor in a patch, a long strip of rectangular light.

The truth dawned on him. His imagination was revisiting his release from prison after he had been arrested the first time, as a member of the Pan-Africanist Congress. He had been in prison for only a short time. He was not married then. And Thandi was his wife's name; he was seeing Thandi before they were married.

He smiled at the thought. His mind was not creating stories, not altogether; it was revisiting the past. He liked it. He liked everything about it. He allowed himself to be taken back again. In his mind, he went back to the department store, Bekimpi–Zweli in the department store. The whole thought of being out of prison was very good.

Yes, he had found the record-book inside his pocket. But then it happened again. Someone ate half his buttered bread in the canteen. He felt very hungry when he found this had happened. He said loudly: 'That's the trouble of working with so many people. Nothing is ever all right.' Later he found it was his cousin who had eaten the bread. He kept his mouth shut again, in case it became a public joke.

102

Days passed, months passed. One day he sat counting his pay. He was happy. He reviewed his life in the department store: 'So this rational being is an ordinary human being after all. He wanted to be rational, but when confronted with the realities of life he was as grossly irrational as anyone.'

He laughed over the idea, and at this moment his mother came in, to find him laughing by himself.

'Wo, my son, you will go mad. I told you not to read so many books. They are no good. Look at Mr Bambino. He picks up papers now wherever he finds them. He is filthy and behaves like a pig. No one can believe that he was once a lawyer.'

He knew there was no truth in the story that that imbecile, now mentally deranged, had ever even been to school. He teased his mother:

'Ma, next year I am going to the university.'

'No, no, my son. Don't you hear what I tell you?'

He laughed and went to his room. The Saturday afternoon was gloomy. Next day it would be Christmas Eve. Two friends called in. They were very dunk. 'These fellows are on the way to becoming alcoholics,' he thought.

'Hello, you old punk,' one was shouting. The other came forward to hug Zweli. He pushed him away and broke free.

'You smell like a lavatory. I wonder what woman would kiss you. You smell terrible.'

'Oh, don't worry, this is the smell of a man. It's what girls like. Come on, Zweli, come and smell like a man. Take some of this.'

He pulled a bottle of some home-made concoction from his back pocket. Zweli decided to go to his room. One fellow followed him; he shut the door in the drunkard's face.

After a long time, he could see that the drunkards did not want to leave; they were playing records. He sneaked out of the back door and went away.

The rattle of keys broke into Bekimpi's daydream. A warder said 'Come'. He stood aside, and Bekimpi came out of the cell. He walked down the smoothly polished floor. His face shone redly in the floor. Before him a convict was sliding on a cloth, shining the floor. He slid

103

from wall to wall in the wide passage. He did not stop for Bekimpi and the warder to pass, but timed their approach and slid to one side while they passed, and then slid back again without having to lose his rhythm.

The passage was in the centre of these kulukudus, so that it was in the shade. At the turn of the passage they came into the burst of light coming in from a side door. They passed the door and came into the clearing. Men who were in solitary confinement worked on the small black stones, crushing them even smaller. They all turned to look at him. Most of them had already declared him a sell-out. He looked at them only once as he passed by.

'That one has gone to pot,' one whispered.

'And that's a bloody damn leader. Selling out,' another whispered.

'That shouldn't surprise you. How many leaders have sold out now? And we rank and file remain staunch.' There was contempt on the man's face.

'Who said Bekimpi has sold out?' another asked angrily. 'Don't talk about things you don't know anything about.'

'He has. What are all these ups and downs to the offices?'

'He has not. That's not evidence of selling out.'

'It is. Or Van der Merwe would have given up long ago. There's something big that they want from Bekimpi. And they're getting it. The whole Underground outside will be dug out sooner or later, you listen to me.'

'You're talking shit,' the other shouted. The warder, watching them, stepped nearer.

'He talks alone in the cell, believe me. Like a madman.'

'What does he say?'

'God knows. Gibberish.'

Bekimpi stood in the office before Van der Merwe. The sight of this man always brought Bekimpi's mind into full operation. He was at war with this man, and he had to be careful.

The inspector eyed him happily, and said: 'You could be out of prison by now. You could be happy with your children. I didn't think you were such a big fool.'

He waited. Bekimpi said nothing.

'Do you want to see your family? Bring those photographs, Du

Plessis . . . look here: your child, completely neglected. Look how the disease is eating his skin. The whole body, filled with blemishes. It's high time you took care of your children, they're half-starved.'

Bekimpi heard these words and saw the photo. He wanted to be cut off. He wanted to be aloof and feel nothing. In a moment he was cut off. The child in the photograph became just another child, any child in a picture magazine–one of those children wasted by malnutrition and disease. Such as the starving children of the Congo, for whom he felt no direct stab of pain, but merely disgust at the depravity of mankind.

In this state of mind he was taken back to the cell.

Thabo's Song to Sobukwe

We heard rumours of the condition of Bekimpi in solitary confinement, and stories about his selling out. Silent in our cell one evening, we were ready to listen to Thabo. His face was worried. I knew he was thinking about Bekimpi. As he spoke, his voice quivered:

Sobukwe,
Haven't we missed a vital point?
Why are we reluctant to follow your lead?
You, who never pushed us from the rear,
But led us from the front,
Like the good shepherd.

Why are we reluctant to follow your lead?
Don't we want the freedom that you want?
We want it.
Do we like to live a slave life?
We don't.
So why the hell
Are we reluctant to follow your lead?

Sobukwe,
Haven't we missed a vital point?
In the outbreak of the thunderstorm
We shivered:
And we could not analyse the cause of its outbreak,
We could not understand the phenomenon
Of its electric charge.

And we watched the thunderous storms
Of the Island gathering death,
Collecting mist and fog in their wake,
Sweeping Antarctic winds of cold
With the clap of the thunderous hands of death
Collecting gales and dregs and crushed sea-shells—
All to crowd your little white-painted hut,
Moaning against your dedication to free
The people you consider your countrymen,
The people that are reluctant to follow your lead.

Are we offering you up
As a sacrificial animal
To appease the unknown gods,
That dare to accuse us of disloyalty?
The ancestor who died without a goat
For us, that are living, to inherit,
But now demands a goat from us as an offering;
The ancestor that left us in poverty,
But now demands that we slaughter six cows for him;
Demanding that we offer you up to the oppressors'
    hatchet?

Sobukwe,
We have pushed you to self-immolation
For our sake, haven't we?
Even in the outbreak of the thunderous storm,
That banished any ray of the sun there,
Leaving the whole of the Island grimly overcast,
Your little white-painted hut glittered;

It glittered with your undaunted courage;
It glittered with your unwavering hope;
It glittered with your unflinching determination;
It glittered with your unsagging morale;
It glittered with your uncowering convictions;
It sparkled with your unerring aspirations;

It sparkled with your irrefutable principles;
It sparkled with the love of your mind,
It sparkled with the power of your ability.

We all looked to that little hut
For rededication and hope.
Your convictions and principles
Were never a reproach to you,
Or to us.
And by them you intend to die.
Does the world know you are in Robben Island?
But what's that to them? They can go and eat dung.

But, Sobukwe,
We have missed a vital point.
Why are there traitors among us?
Our brothers who sell out to our enemies,
Our brothers who stand in the witness-box,
Not by an error of knowledge,
But by a breach of morality—
That today peace has been faked by the muzzle of a gun,
Cowering us all into lethargic harmless grinning kids;
That today they scream in mirthless joy—
There is peace in South Africa!

No, Sobukwe,
You are not a sacrificial animal.
Yours is an act of knowledge and conviction,
An outright rejection of the slave-life,
A yearning for personal freedom.
And in the effort of freeing your personal self
Knowing that every one of us, a slave of the status quo,
Must rally behind your banner,
And, in a concerted action against a common enemy,
Fight together.

Some have screamed that the slave-era
Ended with the American Civil War.
Did they notice that besides physical enslavement
We witness in the twentieth century
Mental enslavement
And spiritual enslavement?

But, Sobukwe,
Unless we realise, as you did,
That our personal freedom, which is usurped,
Is our prime instigation,
We shall turn traitor in dangerous moments.
Unless one realises that it is not
The freedom of the next man
But his own that is his prime motivation,
He will retrace his steps back to bondage
In the outbreak of the thunderous storm.

Oh, Sobukwe,
This is the vital point we have missed.
We are reduced to the futile argument:
Why must I die while so-and-so
Remains to eat the fruits of freedom?
We are reduced to a state of self-preservation
Because we do not realise whom
We are fighting to liberate.
We don't realise that it is not
Self-sacrifice for the sake of another,
But for one's own personal freedom
Which has been usurped.

Oh, Sobukwe, we will say
We are fighting for the masses,
But when one is in the claws of the oppressor
He forgets the masses and thinks of his own skin.
If the masses benefit when one fights

A personal struggle in concert with others
Against a common enemy,
This is the ultimate state to be wished for.

This is a struggle for those who feel personally enslaved;
But we are reduced to the state of the American soldier
    in Vietnam,
Who is fighting a foreign war.
No personal freedom of his is flouted in so far a country;
He fights with a groaning heart,
And if it were not for military orders
He would desert.

That is the vital point we have missed.
We are reduced to cowards
By the error of our ideas;
We hold that we are sacrificing ourselves for someone
    else
Instead of for our personal freedom.

And in the light of these things,
The basis of our convictions is misconceived.
Unlike you, we wanted to reverse the law of cause and
    effect.
The cause of the struggle is enslavement;
The effect of that struggle is victory or defeat.
We find ourselves moved by the effect, the hoping to win,
Instead of accepting hope as positive to the goal,
Since despair is negative to the goal.
When we plunge into the struggle on that premise,
And dark clouds of repression settle over our heads,
They blot out the ray of hope,
And what we are left with is—no motivation; despair
    and frustration.
Then we find ourselves marching backwards,
Or turn outright traitors.

Mostly it is opportunists who do so,
But are we not all opportunists?
But if we find ourselves moved by the pain of
    enslavement,
And are not willing to endure it any more,
Let the dark clouds settle:
They will only mean extra motivation to act.

One can't realise this until he realises
That the cause strikes the self, in painful stabs,
And is felt by the self only;
He can't feel it for someone else.
But you, Sobukwe,
Are a ray of light to which we must all look.
Oh, that many Sobukwes were born;
How many strong men have there been?

Old Man Mashamat

My mind was singing nice happy thoughts as I went by pushing the wheelbarrow. I was carrying stones to the crushers. The memory of a jazz festival was still sweet in my mind, like the last gulp of ice-cream flowing down the throat. The festival had come upon us three days before, like a deluge on drought areas. It was not a thing organised by the warders for the whole jail, but by us amaGoha, while the others were out at work. This was at the time when the quarry span was halved, one half remaining indoors. Now D section was to have its own show on the following day, Thursday. It was thinking of this that made me feel happy.

I had come on a visit to the quarry. It was difficult to infiltrate into the small spans of twenty or twenty-five, because the span warder knew all his men. But the big span, with more than five hundred, was easy; no one knew them all. Besides, the big span accepted all stray men with no other place to work. It was also a place for demotion and punishment; a man would be expelled to the quarry. If he left the small span, his absence was conspicuous; but we always told the warder that he had been sent to the kulukudu for meal-stops.

Old man Mashamat (a name abbreviated from a long, unpronounceable Pedi word) sat on a huge brick wearing gauze-wire goggles that made him look like a motor-bike rider. He sat crushing the slate-black stones small, and the small stones even smaller. Old Mashamat: grey as ash, green as summer vegetation and black as the stones he was crushing. It was the gleam of a black face shining like tar in the sunshine, washed by the bitter sweat that oozed out with the over-exertion of his body, and flowing down his hairy chest till it looked like a wet raincoat. He sat in the second row of men, lost among the bouncing hammers let down by springy hands in efficient

112

blows, crushing the black stones small and the small stones even smaller.

Five rows of white-jacketed men, all motor-bike riders; rows of thirty or thirty-five men, business-like men with flying hammers. They sat on bricks. Around them were uncrushed black stones: in front of each was a heap of crushed stones that every moment became thicker and higher than the largest ant-hill; and every moment the reflex hand came down forcefully with the hammer on the stones. Each man sat quietly, unidentifiable from the rest, each one bent, hunched up, listening to the ratter-tatter music of his hammer and those of the others, crushing the slate-black stones small, and the small stones even smaller. On went the rat-tat, ratatat, rat-tat-tat tat, louder as I came nearer. And I could not see old man Mashamat until I stopped in front of him, as he asked me to give him some of the stones I had in my barrow. Huh, it was the very man I wanted. I laid the barrow to rest.

The scene was in the quarry. This was the stone industry of the Island. They used the stones to build more jails. The old man Mashamat: big and stout, huge and tall, twice my size. And as I was in my early twenties, he was about three times my age. Big and stout, with a hefty stomach that defied hunger to make it subside.

'Ah, moshimane, lad, it is you?' he said, recognising me.

'That's me, dad. Life is treating you well?' I said. We were talking in sePedi. I was able to talk to him for just as long as I was off-loading the stones. A military cap was walking up and down not far away, and convicts were howling at some men who were doing the same job as me.

On a second time round I managed to say: 'Dad, I want to come to D section today.' He knew what I wanted. He just looked at me with blank eyes, and did not wait for an explanation.

He said at last: 'Hei, moshimane, you want me to get arrested?'

He looked at me with a glittering purple eye, his thick lips puffed.

'You've already been arrested, dad. Long ago.' I should have felt guilty, taking advantage of an old man; but it was not Mashamat's way to encourage us to think he was old. He wanted us to meet him on the same terms in which we dealt with each other, we the young men. There was no diplomatic pretence, or accommodating to the

113

feelings of one another. It was plain friendship, that calls a spade a spade. It was not for him to trade in euphemisms, as long as the particular thing said was not an insult. He was strong, and had proved that he could be like us, and even beat us.

'Would you take my meal-stops for me, eh? Moshimane, eh?' he said, almost shouting, his eyes laughing in triumph for throwing that idea at me.

'Get moving there!' shouted the warder. I moved on and gave stones to the others. I was pushing a wheelbarrow with a rubber wheel. It felt very light in the firm grip of my small hands. And for a time I was not aware of it. I just pushed, pushed in the way an eye can be focused, but not see anything before it. There were many dreamers on the Island, but I reckon I was the worst, when I was in a nostalgic mood. See a man being a lone driver of a barrow among a host of other drivers; see him mouth-locked in a company of pick-swinging men, while the others sing; see him behind the giant chisel, wielding an eight-pound hammer—see such a man, and know that he is the king of his castle suspended in mid-air; he is leaning on the window of the balcony, viewing the open sea of the blue sky. See such a man crouched down in hot sunshine, like a wet rooster, crushing the stones small, and the small stones even smaller; see him with a shovel scooping earth, silent among talking men, some of them discussing subjects from the lofty tower of philosophical thought while they work; see him doing any dirty piece of Island work with an introspective look on his face—and know that he is lying at home enjoying the nearness of his family, or that he is walking down the main street of his home town, or window-gazing in the shopping centre, or at other times he is grappling with the forces of oppression: he is a hard puncher in a ring, facing the monster called white domination.

The sky before me was bluer than the blue-seal which the washer-woman uses for white linen. And the blue of the sky intermingled with the blue of the sea. Each blue swallowed the other blue in the instant of my observation, merging into a spread-out stratum of blue without dimension, without texture, yet not amorphous. The horizon implanted itself there the moment I focused my eye, and before I could retract my gaze, it had created an opaque glass I could not see

114

through. I pushed into the quarry. I pushed out of the quarry. I delivered stones to the crushers. I did this almost unaware of it all. I did not worry about the old man. I knew our business was settled.

Jail teems with evil—my mind went on—it is infested with the germs breathed out by the devil himself. It ferments with ferns and fungus feeding on the tender tissue of the heart. 'Come on, poqo, come on, poqo, come on, poqo, come on . . .' went the endless yelping of a military cap; 'work hard, work hard, hard, hard, hard, don't be lazy,' bleated the incorrigible convict, determined to outdo his master. There was a time when the Emperor Haile Selassie of Ethiopia annoyed the white man, from the special-branch man to the warder. He had disillusioned them with their belief in him as a good, moderate, untroublesome African. For some time they had been spitting his name at us: the old jackal of Addis Ababa.

Such was jail. It reeked of evil. If you opened your eyes, you could see it—a cryptogenic mass, worse than parasites. Prick your ears more sharply, you could hear it whining more painfully than a mosquito in the region of your ear. Clear your nostrils, you could smell it, more pungent than ether, a vomit-agent like the lav bucket full to the brim. But this was a raw Island. A colonial institution like a jail does reform, like any other institution. But it has limits, arresting its reform at an embryo stage. And since it started a million miles behind other institutions, and stopped before it started, it had hardly changed at all. If it did reform, it was at the cost of flogging and kicking the jailed; starving them, and sapping their energy by compelling them to do beastly tasks. When bashed, the jailed turned the other cheek; when hungry, they went on hunger strike; when cold, they flung their jackets away. To reform the world, Christ had to climb Calvary. Since the world is still as evil as Christ found it, what success have the jails had? But in reforming the jail the jailed knew that it was an act more of necessity—with no hope of success—than of will. Because there is nothing to reform, can you talk as if there is an element of good? The system is based on no morality; how can they know that what they do is right? The jailer does not seek change there, because he has no conscience but lives on whims.

On this day when I pushed the wheelbarrow, evil had agreed to a temporary cease-fire. All over the trouble-spots of the world, such as

115

Vietnam, evil agrees to a truce at Christmas, just to flatter Jesus Christ—so much for the believers. Even in jail they allow us a happy Christmas time. The location thugs and gangsters do better: they regard Christmas Day as a day to plunge a knife into someone's bosom, so that for fear of thuggery and gangsterism the people dare not go out. That is what they do in our locations; because they recognise no necessity to convince anyone that they are saints on Christ's day.

I pushed my barrow, happy with the thought that there was going to be a concert in D section. It was all fixed. Old Mashamat had agreed. He would go and sleep in C1, in my cell. I would sleep in his cell. I knew that it was risky. But that was the only way we could do it. And if I had not done it first, someone else would have approached the old man. I felt guilty of taking advantage of the old man; yet old men did not give a damn for music. I wondered what relieved their overburdened minds. Mashamat used to laugh every time I asked the question. You see how stupid our captors were; they knew we were changing places with one another, but they could do nothing about it, because they could not see the individual behind the black sheath of pigmentation. A herdsman is better, since he knows every cow in the herd.

This show was in D3. I had come specially for the 'hit group' there. But impromptu combos were also organised. It was really something when strong groups of the various cells were competing. This used to happen when the big span was reduced in numbers. Then about two hundred who remained behind were locked in one or two cells, while the rest were out at work. It so happened that there was a shortage of work on the Island; and the warders got tired of making us dig trenches in order to fill them up again, or plough useless tracts of land with picks. Then it sometimes happened that the warders went out on military training, and there were not enough left to guard us at work. On such days we had concerts, we who remained. Why shouldn't we? We didn't give a damn for the yells that we should stop. Those who could time it well could always remain behind, because the head-warder of the big span would cut the line in different places on different days, just to trick us. The amaGoha, the strategists, could figure out beforehand where he would cut it. And it so happened that

116

most of the choir groups were amaGoha. So we had nice free holidays with music, to the consternation of the warders. Sometimes we felt that we were cheating the others, the ones who were not strategists, but we were consoled by the fact that most of them liked going out, because they did not want to become soft again. They wanted to remain hard as long as they were there.

It was damn nice in that cell. We let our mouths go running, and to stop ourselves talking we sang. The Summitones, the best combo group on the Island, would give us the latest hit; then The Islanders would come on, another magnificent group.

Old Mashamat was an inspiration to most of us. An old man that did not care about suffering: was this true of us? An old man that did not care about being in jail; was this true of us?

'These old men have lived a long time. They have lived a full life, and now they don't care about dying,' a young man would say, happily, without malice. Mashamat would smile down at him, because these were the terms of discussion he liked. He did not want pity splashed on his face. We found that his attitude was not a weakness of some sort, but an earnest desire to boost our morale.

I could remember him running fast for his dish at Leeukop, when we went for our food. I had stayed with the old man all the way to the Island. And I had met many old men behind bars. In 1963, the Special Branch had collected all the old men who had been active in the politics of the twenties and thirties. They were locked up under the 90-day detention laws. And when they picked up Father Blaxall, I knew that no old man was safe in this country.

Most of them had their cases withdrawn. But old Mashamat belonged to the old politics as well as to the present; and that is why he had a spirit that never sagged.

Bekimpi's Dream: Nompi

Bekimpi paced the little cell in a far-away state of mind. 'So they say my family is in need of me,' he said to himself. 'My family, my children, are in dire need of me.'

He approached the bucket, stood and stared at the contents, then turned away sharply, his teeth stuck together, suppressing vomit.

'That is a bad sight,' he said to himself. 'And that stuff comes from my stomach. From whom else? I'm alone here. Gaboom mealies make very bad shit. My stomach is rotten. If I farted, people might think it was a poison-gas explosion. My bloody family in bloody need of me. So what? The nation is also in need of me. My wife, my children . . . I don't need a Boer to tell me that. There's Zweli, about to leave prison. My time will come too. Why hurry? I have been thinking of my wife the whole day, and yesterday. Why, Thandi's my wife, of course; and this damn Zweli was myself too, of course. But what about Nompi, the girl I nearly married? I'll meet her as Zweli: Bekimpi alias Zweli alias Izwelethu . . .'

. . . He wandered aimlessly towards the street that joins the Hectorway. When he got to the Hectorway, he decided to visit his sister-in-law. He was two days out of prison, after he got a discharge. Mike's wife Selina was acclaimed as one of the most beautiful women of the location. She had a deep liking for Zweli. She would listen untiringly to his complaints. She was twenty years old, and thus younger than him. He went to the back entrance and knocked.

'Come in.' He did not recognise the voice. It sounded very sweet to his ears. Or perhaps to his imagination.

'Come in,' the voice called again. He stepped forward, realising that he had hesitated while thinking about that voice that had said 'Come in' for the second time. He went in.

118

He got a shock; for a time it was as if he was blinded. Selina sat near the fire, smiling at him. She was beautiful, smiling. Her hair was long. Next to her sat another beauty who looked very much like her. 'But surely that sweet voice did not come from this one. It must be the third one.' He stole another look at that one as he sat down. He was dazzled. He forced a smile and greeted everyone. He looked at Selina appealingly, but she only smiled at him. He stole another glance at the third girl, but this one was intercepted; he blushed. The girl looked away and went on with her work, washing the dishes.

At last Selina came to his rescue: 'Zweli, this is Dora, a staff nurse at the Baragwanath hospital, my elder sister.' She was pointing at the one sitting next to her. This was not the one he most wanted to know, and it seemed an age before the girl washing the dishes was introduced to him.

'And this is Nompi, my youngest sister.'

He took that opportunity to look at her, and thought: 'This is Selina at fourteen, it must be.'

She smiled at him. 'Heyi,' Zweli exclaimed, but in his thoughts only. It is a Zulu exclamation meaning nothing in particular, but expressing wonderment and admiration in general. Zweli did not say it aloud, but it showed on his face. His body jerked like a spring, as if he had been pinched on the buttocks. Everyone saw it, and they smiled at him.

'Dora, Nompi: this is Zweli, Mike's brother by the younger son of Grandpa. He was in jail when you last visited us.'

Selina's family lived in the Reef. Zweli had never heard much about this family, and he had taken no interest in it. In any case, Mike and Selina had been married about four years ago, and during much of that period he had been in jail. He greeted the young lady again. When she replied, it was in the same voice that had said 'Come in'. He was thrilled by it.

'I'm glad to meet you, young lady,' he said, as he offered her his hand. A very small hand, and delicate, but capable of generating an electric impulse that left his body shaking. He saw that everyone was looking at him.

He said: 'Don't mind me. I'm feeling topsy-turvy today. I thought

119

I'd fortified my heart against surprises of any sort, but just now surprise has befuddled me.'

'What surprise are you talking about?' Selina asked.

'Oh, let's cut it out.' He sat on the chair.

'Why don't you take my hand too?' Dora asked teasingly.

'Oh, I'm sorry,' he said, standing up again. He was very angry with himself at this early betrayal of his feelings.

'So this is the famous Zweli,' Nompi said, as she found a chair and sat down.

'What do you mean? I don't understand,' he protested.

'I knew you three years ago,' she said.

'You mean she told you about me,' he said, indicating Selina.

'No. Wait a minute.' She went into the bedroom and searched for something. She came back. It was a photo. She handed it to him.

'Where did you get this?' He did not remember giving it to Selina. It was his photo all right.

'I got it from Pegi.' That was a bombshell he had not expected.

'When did you take it from her, and how? And why?' he smiled.

'I stole it from her. Four years back. I was twelve then. She did not suspect anything. Later she lost it for good. Why did I do it? I wanted to see you. Please don't pursue the question.' She smiled, looking at him sideways.

'Devil,' he said to himself, pretending to look at the photo. 'Pegi was a kind of Liz Taylor. I couldn't help myself, with her. She was too cute.'

Pegi lived in the same township as Nompi. He had met her during a school visit to that township.

'Nompi, please take me into your confidence. What prompted you to take the photo from Pegi, and to keep it?' he asked.

'I couldn't understand it myself. I was twelve at the time, so please don't misinterpret it.' She smiled at him. 'What I do know is that Selina talked too much about you every time she visited us, and the result is I know you as well as she does.'

After a while, he decided not to overstay his welcome, and, despite Selina's protests, he left.

120

All the way home, his head was in a state of agreeable turmoil.

He went to his room. He shut himself up in his thoughts: there she appeared glittering in beauty, and that imaginary woman who had haunted his mind faded away. 'I must have light. Up to now my life has been an excursion, a timeless trip into the unknown. All the time I was forlorn, regarding myself as a victim of life, a victim of repression, a victim of denied love and a victim of melancholia. I turned my back on the miseries of life, and nursed love in the hope that it would be the joy of my life. Instead, it hurried me into the abyss of the condemned. But you, my Nompi, must be my light. Or, if love is a killer, let it make a swift job of me so that I dissolve quickly and make my absence from this world permanent. But there I see you still, smiling at me. You give me strength; I feel it. Tomorrow I will feel a new man. Now I can feel the effects of love. Of course it is all in the mind: love has changed my state of mind. From looking on the gloomy side of things, I look on the brighter. I banish my nervous disorders.'

When he woke up in the morning he was elated. He could not conceal it; everyone noticed it, and he did not care. Last night he had gone out like a candle and slept soundly. The next day would be Christmas Eve.

The morning air was cool. He took a lazy walk across the street into the golf field. He kicked the dew, which was late to vanish with the sun. He kicked it until his shoes were soaked to the socks inside; they were only morning slippers. He tried to rationalise his feelings towards Nompi. He had the strength to do so because Nompi herself had revived him. He muttered to himself: 'It is true that yesterday I was submerged in a boiling pan of emotions. I can trace that to Nompi . . . she produced a condition in me where my emotional ferment overcame my rational judgment of her. She is not to blame. I was already an emotional mess, corpuscles seething as they invaded the peace of my heart. There are ghosts, witches and fiends in prison that make one's blood shiver; green-eyed monsters taking the shape of massive rats that haunt a man out of his wits, and leave him emotionally squeezed dry. I met Nompi at a time when there was a deep

121

yearning in me, a yearning for a lover who would satisfy my description of the ideal woman. I love Nompi but I know too little about her. The very fact that I loved her at first sight rang the alarm-bells. I must give it time, time to prove itself; time to mature to true love. Who says I am going to marry her tomorrow? Nor must I assume that Nompi is the mythical girl who has haunted my imagination. True, my imagination has already claimed that it is so. Here are Nompi and Thandi: it is unfair for me to ask why I prefer Nompi to Thandi. Since I do not love Thandi, to hell with all her values and qualities. I do not know Nompi's inner qualities; I know Thandi's; but in qualities visible to the eye Nompi excels, seen through the goggles of love. But if reason tells me she is not the right woman, then love can go hang itself. I am prepared to flatter Nompi with all the rosy fibs of courtship, because those are what some women like. I must tell her a nice-sounding rosy fib even if it means I must mention the fantastic woman who was pestering my imagination. I know that all this time I have been living with a hallucination; I must tell Nompi that it was she, the nymph of my imagination, that was giving me sweet dreams. I will leave it to her to believe it or not.'

When he discovered he was at the end of the golf course, he turned back. There was no dew to kick now, so he kicked the air, missing the grass, as he walked down the field in a happy mood.

The idea that prisoners come out of jail with shattered morale is far from true. Yet with Zweli there was a cold breeze of utter dejection, a damnable sense of having failed to live up to his convictions and aspirations.

In this short period he saw much of Nompi. She was very light in complexion. Her hair was just like Selina's; when she had done it up it looked like a wig. Her face had a smiling charm; one would never tire of looking at it. Her eyes were engaging, looking at him under her lashes. She had just taken the J.C. examination and was awaiting the results. She was the kind of girl that had to be escorted to and from school because of the wolves who could not restrain themselves.

Christmas night found them sitting on the doorstep of his brother's home, marvelling at the beauty of the moon. Selina was preparing supper. Nompi suddenly touched his hand; a shiver ran up his spine.

122

She smiled at him, and the moon lit up her face. At last he found the words:

'Nompi, my dear, you can read my thoughts as I can read yours. Why must I embarrass you and myself by going into details?'

He paused; she was not looking at him.

'You appeared to me in the form of a woman who came into my imagination and has stayed there ever since. It was a baffling experience; I began to understand it only when you showed me the photograph you took from Pegi. Then the hallucinatory woman disappeared from my imagination and you are there instead.'

'But what about your other girls—particularly Thandi?' she asked.

'Believe it or not, my dear, there comes a time in a man's life when he insists on loving to such an extent that he can't love less. This is so because love is a single-minded emotion that permits no multiple sharing. Unless it has fallen on a selected seed-bed it will not take root, and so it becomes a weak plant, always at the mercy of storms and whirlwinds. It is a yearning passion that demands an ideal partner. Unless such a partner is found, that passion leaves a trail of heartaches and unhappiness wherever it has passed. Love is the expression of one's values; the emotional debt one owes for the happiness he or she receives from the values of another. So I can say emphatically that my love for those other ones you mention fell short of my standards. But in the darkness of a dense jungle, a confused state of love, I have seen a star that can light my way to happiness. You are my star and my light. And I hope that is true for you, because neither of us must love out of pity or gratitude, or for material gain, or the desire for friends and relatives; because love so founded has no affinity with reason, it is built on sand.'

He paused. She looked at him and said: 'I understand what you say. I assure you, my true one, you are my highest value just as I am your highest value. No one will rank higher with me save the Lord, for it is through Him that I have found you, and you have found me. Let me tell you the secret, that I am in a condition as fresh as an unpollinated flower. It may please your conscience to know it. As you know, I am only seventeen. Please be courteous with me, as I am still a virgin.'

She was looking deep into his eyes, and he back at her. He took her

123

into his arms and said: 'Nothing could make me more happy than to know you love me. And I can't say how I feel about what you tell me —I hoped it might be so.'

He kissed her tenderly. It was the kiss he had so much yearned for, and how different it was, how warm; the effects of love. Neither of them heard the door creak open, or saw Selina standing at the door.

'Congratulations,' Selina said, and disappeared behind the door.

The piercing green eyes of the terrifying creatures he could not identify were retreating; they had been crowding in on him, now they were giving way. They left stretching before him a tract of green valley. He suddenly saw in his mind his prison friend, Thabo. He felt he had enough strength to endure the thought of his friend's misery.

'And remember, Zweli,' she said, teasing him, 'I don't mind your hallucinations.'

At that moment Kay drove the Prefect up to the kerb and parked in front of the gate. He got out and approached the two, who had been again oblivious of the world around them. He handed Zweli a sealed envelope, and went into the house. Zweli held up the envelope against the light coming through the window. It was stamped Robben Island. 'Yes,' he said to himself, 'I thought it was—just at this moment when I am having a success with Nompi.'

'Where does it come from?' she asked, as they walked in.

'Makana Island,' he said, opening it.

'Where is Makana Island?'

'It is Robben Island. We have renamed it, after the first victim to be banished in the history of South Africa—Makana the Left-handed. 'I haven't been there yet,' he told Nompi, 'but I have the feeling that I'll follow the others sooner or later.'

He read the letter to himself. Nompi saw the smile on his face wear off. Then he was sweating and breathing heavily. She watched him reading to the end; she was worried.

'He is dead. He is gone,' he said, half shouting.

'Who?'

'Oh, why must it happen at this moment?' he said, laying his head

124

on the table. He pushed the letter across to her. Selina and Kay came in, with curious looks. Nompi read the letter:

Dear Beki,

As you know, Duma was removed from Makana Island to Paarl, because he was suffering from T.B. Then to all our amazement he was brought back, because he is a lifer, they said.

As soon as he arrived, the sickness struck him down. You know there is a monkey at the hospital there, a physician from Cape Town, he tossed him out with a hot clap behind the ear. He had to work at the quarry with us. It was cold that day, and drizzling. We were all wet and cold, but it was worst for the T.B. and asthma cases.

Duma could not take any more. He protested, but he was kicked in the stomach by the Boer Makwarini. He sank to the ground. Later he was taken to the hospital, and he died that night. The post mortem was that he died from decay of the left lung. This letter is being slipped out through our friend, you know him.

Yours known to you
(The Island)

He experienced an undercurrent of violent, seething emotions flooding into his bloodstream. The expression on his face changed from grief to frightening defiance, anger and hate. But after a moment or two he became aware of his helplessness. He wanted to cool down; so he went out. Nompi followed him. He saw the car parked outside, and it gave him an idea. He invited Nompi to get into it with him; the key was in the ignition. They drove off to the outskirts of the location. He parked the car off the road, and they got out. They stood looking at each other; her face was glittering in the moonlight. All was quiet except for the groaning croak of a frog in the distance, and the buzz of a mosquito near by. He felt helpless; he was helpless, yet he felt strength pouring back into him. He declared in his own thoughts: 'Let the martyrs of Africa live in our hearts; there is no cause for remorse. And this girl here is now the strength behind me.'

Taking her into his arms, he said: 'We have come to the stage in our lives which all adults must reach, except those who have given

125

themselves to celibacy. We are travelling along a thorny footpath through the valley of human misery. Snakes and scorpions cross our path. Lions and wolves roar and bark on every side. We look up to the sky, expecting manna to fall from heaven. It does not fall. Instead, the birds of heaven, the eagles and the vultures, snatch the crumbs of bread from our hands. We feel the mosquito bites, bringing the danger of disease. We do not know where we started from or where our destination lies, yet still we are travelling; we were born travelling, and we will die travelling. It is a strange land we are travelling in, and we must stick together like body and soul, for when these part the human being dies. Our ordeal comes from the fact that the green pastures of Africa are no more. How green they were! The grass taller than I am, where the herds of our forefathers grazed; milk and honey in plenty; the foundations of a growing culture. The green pastures of Africa, stretching back to an age before the days of King Shaka; before the voyages round our Africa began. Those days are gone. A love partner for such a journey must be chosen on spiritual and rational grounds, not on material and moral ones, because this is a world that is materially and morally sick.

'My dear Nompi, let us look back to draw strength from our past, for in this lies our security. Nompi, you do not realise what you have done to me. I was finished; I was on the threshold of a nervous breakdown. I love you, Nompi.'

Love whispered in the air around them. Soon each was lost in pleasant dreams, dreams of the future. After a long time they drove home. Neither knew how short their time was; Zweli did not know how precarious were his love, and his new-found strength.

Nompi died on an electric chair at some obscure police station. This was a bitter memory, one of which the mind and heart of Bekimpi were afraid. He sat staring at the door and not seeing it. He perspired black sweat. His hands trembled. The whole weight of this memory, like a big boulder, rolled on him; he squeezed into a corner, but it reached him there. He was like a cornered rat in an empty cupboard, and the memory was a monstrous cat advancing, ready to claw. He did not want to think about Nompi, but this whole review of the past was bringing him to it. The memory came in the

126

guise of hallucination, of daydream. It was the only way it could come, through his struggles to suppress it. He pretended he was Zweli, the Zweli about to leave prison, not daring to be himself. But he had been Zweli right up to the moment of Nompi's death. On coming to the Island he had been surprised to meet a namesake, the man in the third cell. This man, whom he had known slightly in earlier years, had also named himself after that same leader in one of the African states. It revived the name with its bitter memories, the name which Bekimpi had decided to forsake after the tragedy of his girl.

Nompi was taken by the police, who alleged that she was involved with Bekimpi. They wanted to know the whereabouts of Bekimpi, also known as Zweli. Bekimpi had disappeared.

'Don't beat the girl,' a chief sergeant cautioned. 'It is not to be done that way.'

'You're right,' another said. 'We mustn't leave marks on her.'

'The chair will do it.' A man in civilian clothes was speaking. 'That'll make the damn bitch talk.'

'What? Are you mad?' the sergeant almost screamed.

'Don't say I'm mad. This thing can be applied very mildly if one wants it that way. It's safe enough.'

'I say you're bloody insane.' The sergeant was red-cheeked with anger.

'You're talking bullshit. Come, little girl. You're going to talk. Where is Zweli?'

Nompi stood in the corner, hot with tears.

'It's your last chance. Where's that Zweli, otherwise called Bekimpi?'

The man in civilian clothes appeared to be outside the rule of the sergeant. Nompi knew where Bekimpi was, and her refusal to talk got her on to the chair. She was finished by the fear of it before the shock got her. It was something milder than the mild current the man wanted to apply which killed her.

'She should have told them . . . she should have told them . . . she should have . . .' Bekimpi shouted, staring at the door. 'She should . . . the fool. The fool . . .' Footsteps came tramping hard, and passed by his cell.

127

With the death of Nompi, Bekimpi went back to Thandi and married her. He was an ever-wanted man. And this brings to my mind the day I saw him at the stadium, the day of the tornado, the beginning of his real troubles: he was picked up by the Saracens, quite wrongly, and ever since then he had been in and out of prison on political charges. And now he knew he was in for the last time.

'I have a feeling, Nompi, that I will end the way you ended.'

He climbed on the bundle of blankets and looked out of the window. The sun shone through the plantation, on its way down to the sea. From afar he saw white jackets, swinging against the air. The spans were coming in. A cloud of dust arose as the men walked, dragging their feet. They were hungry. They were on the third day of a hunger-strike. I walked among them.

The Hunger-Strike

My arms felt numb and lifeless, as if they were not part of myself. And a kind of morbid discharge oozed from a cut on the side of my left arm. My hands fastened on the arms of the wheelbarrow. And loosened. By willpower they fastened again, but kept losing their grip, to glide warmly down the smooth steel. The steel had acquired a new-iron shine with constant use. Slowly the monster made its way through the reluctant sandy soil. My face was reflected on the shining arms of the wheelbarrow, and my cheeks were coloured by a metallic glint. I looked at my arms and those of the barrow, and found it difficult to discern much difference in size. I had been sapped. Then I fixed my eyes on the far northern horizon. It stretched out indefinitely, appearing to loom above the plantation farther away. It slashed nostalgic wounds in my heart. I immediately turned my eyes to the western horizon. Somewhere the damned sun must find its hole and hide its face from the eyes of mankind, allowing darkness to spread her web-net over the world; so that we might sleep, to rest our wearied muscles. The sun must scram; at least, we on Robben Island did not want it. Its permanent disappearance from this area of the earth would only mean a release. Release—to feel as light as a sponge squeezed of all the water which had soaked it, making it heavy, stale and suffocating. It would mean a mind-easing glide into an ever-spreading vacuum, where the senses—sight, hearing, smell, taste and touch—would achieve a sensuous self-abandonment in a gyrospasmic interplay. The inner sight: in its perfection, a television with which I could scan the landscape of my home town, and see all those I wanted to see. The inner ear: nothing to mar its reception, so that any time I dialled home, the voices of those I wanted to hear would flood my ear-drums. The inner smell, the imagined touch: sailing in a vacuum of make-believe. Then we could bear our empty stomachs with dignity.

Even as I thought of this, my stomach groaned. It groaned with the sickening cry of a muffled dove, invoking my sympathy as if it were a separate entity from me, a something not part of myself, calling for help in the dark. I looked down at it; it had sunk in an inch farther below the abdominal line. I looked at the sun. It was travelling leisurely towards the west; but it was now casting long shadows, falling across the tomato gardens next to us. I cursed.

'That won't help you,' a friend said to me, as he sank the shovel in the heap of earth. His muscles twitched as the shovel came out with a full scoop and he dumped it in my wheelbarrow.

'What won't help?' I asked.

'Cursing the sun.'

'I know it won't help, but the hell with it. It's a collaborator.' I cursed again between clenched teeth. He smiled, and everyone smiled at me as if to offer pity. 'Anyhow, I feel better after cursing,' I said, almost apologetically. They burst out laughing. The warder took a few steps towards us.

'God will not like what you said,' another friend said, wiping sweat from his face with a rag.

'If God is the sun, then he's a collaborator too,' I said, almost shouting.

'Hei, quiet there. Get on with your work!' the warder barked. He was not a bad chap, but he had changed overnight, perhaps by order, since we went on hunger-strike. But did we give a damn?

'The fault, Danny, is not in the stars, but in ourselves,' my friend said.

I looked at him sternly. 'What are you implying? You want to blackleg?'

'No; but I repeat, Danny, the fault is not in the stars, but in ourselves.'

'So noble Cassius would have told noble Brutus. They were speaking of tyranny, remember?'

'It stands to reason who was tyrant.'

'It was Caesar, of course,' I said.

'So, you are Brutus?'

'If I stand on the side of truth.'

'Truth? What truth?' My friend was on the verge of screaming.

'I said quiet there. Bring your tickets.' It was the span warder. The fool. We gave him the tickets, and continued to discuss Shakespeare. What is wrong with the bum, we thought? Doesn't he understand that we are on strike? How can he punish us by hunger when we are on hunger-strike?

We were getting through the third day of the hunger-strike. And now this day was withering too. And we were already thinking in terms of the morrow. Oh, the terrible morrow, another day of buckling knees. Hunger felt like a bundle of washing hanging inside me. I was working in the sweet-potato plots planted for the pigs and us. Our span was the roaming Hodoshe span. The span which took the biggest share of the burden of the strike was the big quarry span. Five hundred prisoners walked to work there with hungry stomachs. They were the most enthusiastic and determined. They suffered most from the causes of the strike, and they languished most from the effects of it. Warders carrying FN rifles, reinforcements from Cape Town, marched outside the fence-tunnel, covering the marching prisoners. Dust-laden red faces, dishevelled hair obstructing their sight, their hands constantly rising to push it back into place; they were angry men with itching fingers which instinctively strayed to the trigger at each spasm of rage, waiting for the order to fire. They were angry at having been ordered to leave Cape Town, leaving their sweethearts for the jungle-land of raw criminals, miles away from civilisation: made to leave by stupid Poqos. They had been told that they were going to shoot rebellious Poqos. The order to shoot did not come. Disappointed, disgruntled and fatigued, they marched along, looking at the prisoners with hatred.

I was in the zinc prison at the time, the temporary cells of the Island. I managed to slip into these cells to take some judo lessons, that is, to try judo again. In return, the man I changed places with wanted the help of a teacher at the University of Makana.

The hunger-strike had a terrible effect on me. It was only a few days since I had been on another spare-diet sentence. During those days of spare-diet I caught some glimpses of Bekimpi, and saw how frustrated he looked. My spare-diet was only three days of punish-

131

ment by hunger. I filled my belly with the unsalted mealie-rice water, to stop my intestines from shrinking. Two or three grains of mealie-rice which by God's mercy had strayed to the bottom of the bowl were a big feast. During the early days of my arrest I could refuse the half-boiled, half-cooked mealies. But times had changed. Jail food so conditions the starving stomach that it can swallow the whole bowl without being satisfied. At first I could not finish a quarter of it; now I could finish the whole of it and want more. My stomach had become like a sponge. Miss one dish if you want to witness the battle of the intestines: writhing and wriggling and twisting like a cornered lizard, growling and groaning and moaning like an angry sea.

Then Bra Styles in the opposite kulukudu, who had completed eighteen days of his twenty-one-day spare-diet, would contrive a pendulum, and swing a bowlful of mealies across the narrow passage. Mealies wrapped in a white face-washing rag that had turned yellow with use and dirt, suspended on shoelaces tied together. He would swing hard, and you would reach out with your stretched-out hand, grab and miss; grab and miss again, and finally clutch at the string, panting, and praying that Oom Jan or 'Klein-baas' Piet would not take a stroll into this passage. If he should—hell. And your stomach groaning like a moocher, for fear this food should be snatched away.

We had also used the swinging-pendulum trick at Kroonstad, until 'faithful' Mr Khoza strayed into the passage during his evening patrol around the prison after lock-in hours. He caught red-handed two political prisoners exchanging food for tobacco from the criminals in the opposite cell who were on spare-diet. Tobacco was another commodity as valuable as gold among smokers. But it was a plentiful article among the criminals, who had no difficulty in smuggling it in. Yet Khoza did not smash the racket; it was a jail-bird who ended the trade by sending across a cloth containing sand instead of tobacco in exchange for the food of a political prisoner.

Bra Styles was in for a criminal offence, but was charged while in prison with being a Poqo. With his help, I somehow survived that spare-diet, at the pain of his own stomach. But Styles's offer was not to be refused. I had brought down punishment by hunger on myself when I tried to dodge a small span that was being organised by the new yard head-warder to do a piece of dirty work. A number of those

132

doing short terms were wanted. I attached myself to the big span and told them I was doing ten years.

'Where's your ticket, then?' the head warder asked.

'It's lost.'

'What?'

'Lost.'

'Come on, then. Strip,' he commanded.

Hell. My jacket went and then my jersey. Then it came out as if it was alive, jumping from my sleeve, and dropping at the warder's feet.

Someone said: 'We're starving here; and that's no joke.' And indeed it was no joke. I had never thought until I went to jail that I would be reduced to a state when I would wrangle about food. A state when the arbitrator of disputes was the stomach; when the loudest and most influential part of myself, in all circumstances, was the stomach. We had the same full power of thought as before, but now it was channelled towards satisfying the riotous stomach.

'This is monstrous. This food wouldn't satisfy a cat.'

'We work hard here. In order to work, a man needs energy.'

'They mean to kill us slowly. I'd rather die by one stroke than be strangled slowly.'

It was a constant chorus: in the cells, in the fields, in the spans. The newcomers were hard at it. The older inhabitants merely smiled; some egged us on, others voiced caution. They had complained and complained, but it seemed they were complaining to a mule that had straddled a busy street and wouldn't move. Now they had grown used to the sight of their dry skins.

'It's action that talks loudest.'

'Why should you think the Boers give a damn whether you starve?'

'Why you failed, you people, is because you were afraid to act.'

So spoke the newcomers. But the old-timers had come fresh to the Island once, long before we did.

We were pushing trolleys, running on little rails. We loaded them with sand, pushed them up a slope and dumped the sand on level ground. We had heaped up a hillock of light cocoa-brown sand. What we were building I could not tell: an aquarium? absurd. A swimming pool? not in this way. A prisoner is not told what he is

133

doing. They tell him: Hei, pick up that brick. He picks it up. Hei, come along with it. He comes along with it. Hei, put it there. He puts it there. Hei, run for another one. He runs for another one. After a week he finds he has built something as big as a little kennel for a puppy. So what could we be doing, pushing these monstrous trolleys up and down; little tunnels were dug and filled with little stones, drainage was contrived and bricks were laid. It was long after the hunger-strike that it became clear that a tennis court for the warders had been built there.

It was justifiable for the Islanders to grumble. We ate at half-past six in the morning; by seven we were at work. By nine I was half dead with hunger. And lunch would be at one in the afternoon. We ate lunch back at the cells; this meant we had to drag our fatigue-stricken bones back to the yard. The days dragged along slowly.

One day M. went for a Poqo who worked in the kitchen: 'Hei, why are you so fat when the rest of us are lean? You're eating our food, in the kitchen.'

This was a very audacious attack on a fellow Poqo. It happened in other prisons where the cooks were criminals; but on the Island at that time there were few criminals in the kitchen. So what was wrong? We smuggled one of our men into the kitchen to check the rations; the Poqo there helped him with it.

'It's not the kitchen fellows,' he reported. 'The Boers must be doing it.'

An old inhabitant said: 'Didn't you know that the field head-warder feeds pigs with our food, up at the vineyard?'

'Why didn't you say so before?' someone snarled.

'I thought everybody knew. You watch them, every Wednesday.'

One of us, M., stood before the colonel during inspection of the cells. We were all in newly cleaned clothes. We lined up against the walls of the cells, forming a rectangle of white jackets standing stiff like Napoleon's guard of honour.

'We are starving here,' said M. to the colonel.

The thin lips stretched and then twisted into a wry smile: 'Who are you? The spokesman of the Poqos? You are a leader?'

'No, sir, I just mean . . .'

'Don't you sir me. Do you think I am sir'd by baboons?'

He looked hard at M.; M. returned the gaze and held it.

'Why do you say we? Why don't you say I?'

'Well, I'm not alone in starving.'

'Watch out, young man. Watch out. That's incitement.'

He started to go, but the man next to M. stepped forward.

'Colonel, I am starving here.'

He looked at the man, his lips stretched in astonished anger.

'Am I your colonel?'

The man kept quiet. The colonel started to go again. The next man stepped forward.

'Your worship, I am hungry.'

The field head-warder accompanying the colonel burst out laughing, but stopped immediately. The colonel started to move on again, only to be stopped by another man.

'Starving too?' barked the colonel.

'Yes,' the man said firmly.

'What's wrong with the food they get?' the colonel asked the head warder.

'I don't know, colonel. The Poqos eat too much. They scrape the dishes and lick them with their tongues.' He jabbed the man who stood before them with his swagger stick. 'Isn't that so, Poqo? You eat so much, you leave nothing for my pigs. No? What are my pigs to eat?'

The colonel moved on; another man stepped forward.

'You starving too?' the colonel asked politely, before the man could speak.

'Yes,' said the man.

The colonel looked around him at the line of thirty men, and yelled: 'Look here, all of you. If anyone wants to come up with that hunger-starvation nonsense, he'd better keep it up his arse. I'm not accepting that complaint. Understand?'

There was a dull silence in the cell. He moved on. No one stepped out. He went round the line and left the cell. Ours was the first cell he entered; we heard he was angrier in the other cells.

On the seventh night the impending action reached its peak. A sort of hunger-madness intensified the mood that had been gathering strength since the newcomers came, a new draft from the mainland.

135

It was dark outside when I looked through the window into the void. A nocturnal spirit in the form of a shooting-star whizzed past my eyes and disappeared into the nothingness. All was quiet, and we had some business to finish before the curfew bell knelled us to sleep. The night-duty warder, as usual, had quietly given in to some reverie born of torpid boredom, in a distant corner.

The newcomers had been fairly evenly distributed through the cells from the day they came. And the feelings of rage against the conditions here had shaken up the emotions below the seemingly lethargic surface. But in the cell I was in, it was an old-timer who poked his finger through the crust of the cloud which had kept the cramped muscles of the listeners from action. His cream-laden voice kept them spellbound:

'Sons of the soil, it is a basic principle that we don't engage in piecemeal efforts to win our land back. It is a basic principle that we haven't come here to reform the jails; that our greater responsibility lies beyond these walls that encage us. But in order to push along our primary objective, we need energy; and our enemy has seen fit to cut the supply of our energy, seeking to cripple us. He may cripple us not only physically, but spiritually too, and there lies the danger. The bird's wings have been clipped, and it cannot fly. The lame man has had his crutches snatched away from him. But we have to reverse the disadvantage; the lame man is our enemy, and we shall snatch his crutches and beat him with them.'

He paused. A faint, low, crackling sound, barely audible at ordinary times, filtered into our ear-drums, straining to catch every word of the speaker; the noise was caused by the wind sliding through the openings between the zinc sheets, near the door.

'Sons of Africa,' he started up again, in a thick; deep tone, 'I am delighted that our brothers have come to inject militancy into our deadened spirits. I have been patiently waiting for this hour, and I am glad it has come.'

There was a hiss of exclamations after he had spoken. Several others spoke after him. The other cells had their speakers too. While they were speaking, someone was keeping watch on the main gate for eavesdroppers.

The bell rang, and it rang incessantly, as if it would never stop. As it rang, the slogan rang out, more than usually vibrant: 'Izwe . . . lethu!' It might have shaken the night-warder out of his corner, but his ears were used to such sounds, and he always dismissed them as harmless. It was the way we ended our days.

The next thing was that we were pushing the wheelbarrows on empty stomachs. The decision had been taken. Most of us went about it in a leisurely fashion at work, and did not give a damn about threats of further punishment. The warders had gaped in unconcealed amazement when we passed the kitchen window with the dishes. We sneered at it and went to line up in our respective spans. Then their gaping gave way to sneering grins, certain that we would not last out a day. And orders were given to work us like mules, to break us quickly. On the following morning they expected us to call it off, and when we did not they gaped like hens affected by goitre. On the third day their grins contorted to fiendish anger.

At our plot we were required to make a great heap of soil, clearing the ground like a bulldozer. And we levelled the soil somewhere else, for no reason but to break us. Driving the heavily loaded barrows along a sandy path was heavily taxing on our dwindling energies. On the second day I was beginning to feel it, with pains rising up in my stomach and my spine. My knees were buckling, sapped of every bit of energy. We became shorter in speech. That night we lay like fallen lancers lamed by a thrust with the spear. And it seemed that the fleas had sensed danger in meddling with hungry men; they retreated to their most secret recesses.

Speeches to boost our morale were made lavishly in the cells. I did a bit of speaking too, primarily to lift my own sagging spirits. We sang, softly:

> Unzima lonthwalo: the burden is heavy.
> Ufuna amadoda: it needs the effort of men.

We sang it now with better understanding, for truly the task was heavy. We licked at every crumb of salt to replenish our worn bones and keep our eyelids from acquiring a permanent droop. The kitchen fellows levelled the score by stealing salt for us: they were not taking part in the strike.

137

Free people talk of a balanced diet, and spend their money to obtain it, but still complain about its deficiencies—but what about us? We who had lived on third-grade starch for more than two years here; if we had been babies, we would have filled coffins full of kwashiorkor cases. Lying on my hard mat at dawn on the fourth day, with no strength to lift my head, I saw through the window facing me a grouse, or some such bird, with speckled white and grey plumage, feathered to the toes, sitting on the roof of the kulukudu next to our cell. If I had known what the bird was, I might have said it was a bird of evil omen, allowing myself to believe in a thing which I have never believed in before.

We worked. And pushed on, triumphantly. It was on the morning of the fourth day that the top men arrived, to see whether we were still determined to carry on. And we were. We went to our spans confident that something would happen, and it did. Before we had worked for long we were summoned back to the jail. As our span halted at the gate, a cloud of dust approached, whirling yellow skywards—the big quarry span was coming. I had not liked to think how it had been at the quarry during these days. But I was happy for them that it was ended. The white jackets emerged from the dust, also the army of warders, brown in the dust. The spans filled the yard. Excitement concealed our miserable plight and our fatigue. We were instantly dismissed, and went to our various cells. In the cells, the excitement grew even higher, as if it might burst the roof off. The top men went from cell to cell; our complaints were heard with patience. But the method cut off any consultation between cells. So each cell called off the strike on its own. Each time the top men left a cell, the prisoners went for their first meal.

But it was not for an oppressor to take a beating with lowered eyes. Immediately we had swallowed our first meal, ten of us were called to the office. I was one of the ten. This was not unexpected. I had never thought I was militant, even though my friends told me I was. But always, when fire started to burn those who tried to extinguish it with spit, I was sure to be burned. I first made my journey overseas to Robben Island after a hunger-strike, and I was not surprised when now I was whisked off to the kulukudu.

In the kulukudu I climbed to the window and saw Bekimpi exercising in the yard. He was alone, with a warder watching his exercise. It had been decided that he should not come to the yard when the other prisoners were there. He looked as he did in the olden days; he was as I knew him. Walking with high shoulders and lifted head. He walked with vigour and new spirit. I was prepared for this. During the hunger-strike we had received a note from him. He had given it to one of the Rivonia group to smuggle to us. It was a short note of encouragement and rededication. He didn't mention his own plight. Bekimpi was inspired when he wrote that note. The whole idea of the hunger-strike had broken the cage into which his spirit had been pushed. The effect on him was tremendous. We heard that he had reacted to the news with a physical expression of his excitement, bursting with energy in his lonely cell. It broke the hypnotic spell of his tormentors.

By the time I left the punishment cell, Van der Merwe and his special-branch men had come again. The ten of us were moved because of that; we were thought to bring the revolutionary spirit back to Bekimpi. Being back in society elated our feelings. Solitary confinement is bad. But we found the yard warders still in a bad mood.

In the evening, after work, we were searched. The sun was casting long shadows, some of them plastered in giant outlines on the wall facing the west, when men stood next to it.

Most of us averted our eyes from the spectacle next to us. A warder was holding a man by the back of the collar, the whole shirt at the back crumpled into a lump in his enormous hand, and was pushing the prisoner with all his force. The prisoner likewise was resisting with all his strength, his legs geared to a reverse movement but going forward. We heard them growling at each other:

'Wait, man, I will walk on my own.'

'Forward, forward, bloody Poqo.'

'I'm not a Poqo, I'm A.N.C.'

'It makes no difference, bloody Poqo. Forward.'

They went off towards the offices. He was going to be charged for talking in lines. His dish would be food for the pigs. While we stood, others were being searched.

'Stand in line, bastards.'

'Strip, you black thing at the back.'

The searching was done fast, as the warders were in a hurry to knock off. We stood naked in lines, with our clothes and things in our hands. Criminals usually jumped high and turned, bending to show their arse to the search warder. They believed things were hidden in there. When we did not follow this practice, we were always in danger of punishment. We stood in a mass of naked bodies, whether it was hot or cold or raining. There were some warders who could search fast, throwing each garment to the ground as he was handed another to search. We flocked to these quick warders. Others were slow, looking for lice while they searched, to the indignation of the other warders, especially the young ones.

When we approached the dining yard, those who had not been out to work were already sitting there, eating. They sat facing the sleeping quarters.

Before long most of us too had finished eating. We sat still, waiting for the last man to take his food. We were chatting all the time. As more came to sit down the louder became our whispering. We had really enjoyed our meal, because this was meat day; each of us got a piece of pork.

About us were warders, standing or walking around watching us eat. Some were jocular and chatting, others gloomy and impatient.

'You're making a noise. Quiet!'

'Sit on your toes!'

We had sat down flat on the ground, which was covered with the gravel of the slate-black stones crushed in the quarry. The seagulls were flying above us, impatiently demanding our departure so that they could eat too.

'Don't you hear, you bastards—sit on your toes!'

'Don't sit on your arse, you black swine.'

Their voices were like the commotion of sound in a public bar when the drunks all shout at the same time for the attention of the barman. We sat still, but we stopped talking.

'I'll take your tickets, you bloody Poqos.'

'Squat, on your toes. You sit as if you're in your mothers' homes.'

They spoke sometimes to each other, sometimes to us.

'These baboons are cheeky.'

140

'Beasts . . . uncivilised barbarians . . .'

'I'll end up taking their tickets. Hei, damn you, don't you hear? I'll take their tickets, all of them.'

'Bloody Nkrumah, where's Nkrumah now?'

'Man, they don't want to sit on their toes. Hei, you, I mean you, don't look the other way, you, squat, man! You're not in your sitting room. I'm talking to you, look at me when I talk to you, Squat!'

'Rotten communists. Yes, rotten stinking communists. They're communists, these things.'

'They're not communists, they're Poqos.'

'Man, stupid, what difference does it make?'

'They're not Christians. Have you ever seen them going to church?'

'Bloody Ben Bella.'

'Bloody Nasser.'

'And those bloody British are making kaffir states in the protectorates.'

'Kaffir states, bah.'

'English fools.'

'Speak softly, chum.'

'To hell with them, they're only Poqos.'

'Don't worry, Jonathan is a good kaffir.'

'They don't like him, because he's a good monkey. All they want is dangerous monkeys like themselves.'

'We'll shoot them all. They don't stand a chance.'

'What about that kaffir of Bechuanaland?'

'You mean that one that married a white woman, then thinks he's civilised?'

'Oh, Khama's a good kaffir, but I don't like his marrying a white woman.'

'Talk softly, man.'

'Oh, to hell. He's not so much to blame. It's these white communist women. They're a bloody evil, ought to be sentenced to death.'

'What about Swaziland?'

'I don't trust those fools. I think they're Poqos. Communists . . .'

'Speak low, damn you.'

'The colonel said that kaffir in Nyasaland is a good kaffir now.'

141

'The colonel talks a lot of rubbish sometimes.'

'What do you know about it? You're a fool.'

'Yes, he speaks rubbish. I went to a better school than him. Here they don't promote according to education.'

'Don't let the Poqos hear you, man.'

'Man, the Poqos don't know Afrikaans.'

'You're lying. What are they up to in Cell 1?'

'Yes, there's a school. I don't know why they let them study.'

'I told you the colonel is a fool. Study, for Poqos?'

'Yes, Banda is a good kaffir now.'

'That's what I told you, the colonel is a fool. How can a bad monkey become a good monkey?'

'Selassie changed, the reverse of Banda, the colonel says.'

'We helped him against the Italians.'

'That's why I say the colonel knows nothing. Selassie was never any good. What history does the colonel read?'

'He doesn't read history, stupid, he reads politics.'

'Don't call me stupid in front of the Poqos, damn you.'

'They can't hear us, they're too far away.'

'Don't you see that one, looking at us as if he were listening? Hei, look to the front, bastard.'

'Yes, the jackal of Addis Ababa, we helped him against the Italians, then he turns against us.'

'Well, do you trust kaffirs?'

'Yes, why do you trust kaffirs? They never tell the truth. Truth isn't in their language.'

'We should have helped the Italians.'

'Yes, we were fools, how did it happen?'

'It's the bloody English, you know.'

'Yes, the British . . .'

We were listening with interest. We always listened to their politics here when we ate. But on this day they were in full swing. They went on talking while other prisoners came in with their food, and we sat flat on our buttocks.

'These Poqos are listening to us.'

'Damn you, look into your dish.'

'They're still sitting on their arses.'

'Yes, they're stubborn. I'll show them. Squat, fools! Hei, squat!
On your toes! Not on your anus . . . Hei, bloody Poqo, I'm talking
to you. On your toes, jong, on your toes. Bring your ticket . . . and
you, your ticket . . . You, you think you're clever, bring your
ticket . . .'

Before long they had collected about fifty tickets, the jail pass-
books. Then they stopped. There were more than eight hundred of
us, all sitting flat, finished eating.

'Ach, these dirty things, there are too many of them. How can we
punish them all?'

'Yes, it's impossible.'

'Ach, we'll get them, we'll punish them. We'll punish only ten.'

When we were dismissed from the yard, they returned our tickets
and kept only ten. Those ten would be the victims of the warders'
damaged egos.

Bekimpi's End

One day word reached us that Bekimpi was hanging in his cell.

'Dead?' someone screamed.

Further news came. Bekimpi was hanging by the legs, head downward. He had been hung there by Van der Merwe and his special-branch men.

'How could he do it?' Viki said, hardly able to believe it.

'It's impossible. The roof is all concrete,' said another doubter. Then word came that it was not in the cell that he was hanging, but in one of the private offices. There he was hanging, naked.

The inspector came into the torture room. His face was sour and sullen.

'Are you still obstinate?' His voice was raw and savage.

Bekimpi looked at him with his upside-down eyes. He saw murder in the eyes of his torturer. His muscles trembled. The lines of his naked body visibly convulsed. They were lines of straight sinews, oblique and angular. The light from the window shone on his skin, made pale by the cold of two nights. His triceps strained against his ribs; both arms were tied to his body by a rope. His ribs were ugly corrugations, showing up like those of a skeleton in a laboratory.

'Are you still being stubborn?' the inspector repeated. Bekimpi's lips strained to utter one word: 'What?'

The inspector walked nearer and nudged his prisoner's head with one knee. 'I say, are you still being a bloody big fool?' He playfully slapped Bekimpi's sagging buttocks.

'But what do you want from me? You haven't told me,' Bekimpi's voice was hoarse and painful.

'You'll hang here for another two days, or until you die, I tell you.'

Bekimpi tried to follow the eyes of the inspector, but he couldn't.

144

All he could see properly was the roof and the thin rope which supported his body in extreme tension. His eyes were weary of rolling upward to look at the floor. And his neck had strained to breaking point by bending backwards. The floor was two feet below his head.

'I said you are going to play it my way. You are going to work for me,' the inspector said, with a grim smile on his lips.

'But that's meaningless. What do you want me to do?' cried Bekimpi in pain, a twitching backache cutting across his spinal cord. The inspector brushed the prisoner's shrunken stomach. The stomach had been off duty for three days and three nights. The bowels fell down into the chest. The lungs felt that weight, and their own weight crushed on the throat. The wind-pipe was air-locked. Air struggled in and out in hard, panting respiration.

The smile widened on the inspector's lips: 'Many things, of course. Like telling me where is the headquarters of the underground.'

'But you know that. It's in Maseru. You raided that place,' Bekimpi whispered.

'Yes, I know that. That was an office in public, not underground. I mean underground, inside the Republic. You know all these things.'

Bekimpi could do nothing, for nothing of the kind existed. His tongue hung out in despair.

That evening, Du Plessis and two others came to have fun with the hanging man. They let him swing like a hunk of meat in a butchery.

'No, here's better fun: cut the rope with this knife, and see him come down headlong to crash on the floor,' Du Plessis said, and tested the rope with a pocket-knife.

One of them played with Bekimpi's testicles. 'By God, this bastard has a big penis,' he shouted merrily, 'Just like a donkey's.'

Another one slapped Bekimpi's buttocks. Then he took a ball-point pen and pushed it slowly down the helpless man's anus. The muscles there shrank inward like a snail into its shell. Bekimpi moaned.

'Be careful,' Du Plessis cautioned. A brown liquid oozed out and solidified into weak faeces. 'Be careful; the man hasn't been to the lav for three days, remember.'

The one playing with the testicles squeezed harder. Bekimpi

145

emitted a long, painful moan. Mucus and saliva came out of his nostrils and mouth and oiled the floor.

The colonel came and stood at the door, an angry, frightened man.

'Do you want to kill this man? Then don't do it here. Take him to Cape Town.'

Thabo, in our cell, lay flat and breathed with difficulty. The news we had heard had aggravated his T.B. There was silence in the cell; the lights seemed brighter. He trembled out the words:

> How sweet it is,
> Wallowing in the doldrums of irrationality;
> How sugary it is,
> Wallowing in the ammoniac dregs of irrationality.
> It is sweet,
> It is sugary,
> It is honey.
>
> The burning alcohol spirits were never bitter
> For the drunkard to forsake.
> It is heavenly for the pig to wallow in the filth;
> It is heavenly for it to wallow in the mud
> Of its dung and urine and vomit.
>
> How sweet it is
> Wallowing in the doldrums of irrationality.
> The bitch did not mind when it was ravished
> By a pack of dogs.
> Mother-cat never vomited
> When she chewed her only kitten
> And swallowed it.
>
> One man's food is another man's poison.
> Poison it always was, the food of thought,
> For those who do not think;
> For those who think,
> It is bitter,
> It is sour,
> To wallow in the doldrums of irrationality.

146

In the mansion of the whimsical
A woman closed her eyes at midday
And swore to the heavens that it was midnight.
Forbidding his wife to eat eggs—
Eggs a commodity so rare
He wanted to devour them alone—
The man said she would grow horns
If she did eat eggs:
Eggs she had eaten all her life
Before she entered wedlock.
You will be thrown into the bottomless pit,
A father warned his nonconformist son.
Good, cried the son:
For then I will not crush,
I will just fall
Nicely;
Fall and fall
Nicely.

Scientific phenomena in the mansion of the whimsical
Are viewed with awe and lack of understanding.
Reality is dismissed as unreal,
The unreal accepted as real.
A is not regarded as A, but as B,
Or as an irrelevant entity.
Two and two do not make four, but thirteen.

How did they react when Galileo hoisted his telescope
And told them the earth revolved around the sun?
Was it a joke when Archimedes said:
Give me a fulcrum
And a long pole
And a place to stand,
And I will move the world?

Behold, two men rent a house.
The first purchased the property in preparation for his
   marriage,

The second purchased the property for present use.
The groom-to-be placed a new rug on the threshold;
Seeing that it would wear out before his marriage,
He demanded that no one should tread on it.
The other man rightly requested
That it should be removed from the floor.
The groom said it was his right
To place his property anywhere
Because he paid the rent too.

In the mansion of the irrational
Can one find harmony?
When the one thinks positively,
The other thinks negatively,
Or does not think at all, but acts.
There can be no clash of interests
Among the rational:
Rationality being the capacity
To think properly
And act within the scope of those thoughts;
Irrationality being the capacity
To think properly
And act outside the scope of those thoughts,
Or the incapacity to think properly
And act within the scope of those thoughts.

It is sweet,
Oh, it is honey,
To wallow in the muddle of thought;
To go wagging your tongue
About incongruent thoughts.
It is sweet,
Oh, it is sugary,
To marvel at sunken morals;
To feel no shame about it,
To grin idiotically,
When your pet-dog sniffs at your buttocks

When bent to pick up something;
To cackle like an insolent child
At the writhing headless body of a hen
That has just been slaughtered.

One great mind put it:
'Where ignorance is bliss
It is folly to be wise.'
Why not add:
Where irrationality is bliss
It is dangerous to be rational.
The language of exploding dynamite
Became the arbiter against the underdog.
The pigmentation of the skin.
Became the pigmentation of man's mind.
Pigmentation—oh, God has cast a curse upon us.

Cry, O rational men:
Thought is pigmented,
Harmony of interests is sacrificed;
Your inalienable right
To free thought,
To free expression,
To free existence
Within that scope that does not infringe
On similar rights of others
Is usurped.
The right to till the land:
The fertile pastures
Of the coastal lowlands,
Of the inland escarpment,
Of the Limpopo valley,
Of the Vaal valley,
Of the Orange valley—
The right to live in it
Is usurped.

The right to share the wealth of the land:
The yellow metal in the belly of the Reef,
The shining-as-glass metal in the bosom of the Vaal,
The money these materials can buy
By the sweat of man—
Is usurped.

Cry, O rational men
That are the sons of butchers
Eating of the spoils of the butcher,
Sustained by the spoils of pillage
Because by providence you were born
On the fatty side of the status quo.

Rational men
Whose pigmentation is their superiority,
Temporary superiority;
Whose pigmentation is their survival,
Temporary survival—
Cry, O cry
With those whose pigmentation
Is their degradation and their destruction.
For you and all
Are caught in the web-net of irrationality;
For you and all
Are wallowing in the doldrums of irrationality.

Strife and jealousy:
Enemies to prosperity,
Enemies to independent living and pride.
Behold, we live in a world of moral crisis,
As a noted author has said.
But then, if a rational man confronts
With an irrational man,
He has got the choice to avoid the irrational man
Or be swallowed.

But if an irrational man comes to your home
And spits on the threshold,
Or comes and defecates on the floor,
Or urinates in the sink,
In your own home,
To rid yourself of the plague
Bash his jaws or die.
Let not irrationality cling on you
Like an oyster on a rock.
Never live with irrationality
Like a dog lives with fleas,
Or all humanity perishes.
Bekimpi: I am coming with you
To the land of our ancestors.
I know I will not live long.
Report me to our Gods.

It was usual for anyone feeling inspired to address the cell. It was unusual to hear a speech of this kind, which reeked of utter despair. We seemed not to have listened, but we had heard. No one seemed to make any emotional response. Each one was moved by his own speech uttered in silence, of condolence and tribute, and of personal fear.

The next morning the colonel stood at the door of the torture-room. Beside him was Van der Merwe. Bekimpi hung still, cold. The mucus had oozed with foam. The foam came out scarlet with blood. His tongue stuck far out. His eyes were wide and bloodshot. The news had come to us before the actual death this time; it came in horrified panic.

The colonel stood looking at the mess. The inspector stood terror-stricken, unbelieving. The colonel said softly, not looking at the inspector: 'This is your work.'